THE STORYTELLER

THE STORYTELLER

BRANDON HOBSON

Scholastic Press / New York

Copyright © 2023 by Brandon Hobson

All rights reserved. Published by Scholastic Press, an imprint of Scholastic Inc.,
Publishers since 1920. SCHOLASTIC, SCHOLASTIC PRESS, and associated logos are
trademarks and/or registered trademarks of Scholastic Inc.

The publisher does not have any control over and does not assume any responsibility
for author or third-party websites or their content.

Library of Congress Cataloging-in-Publication Data available

ISBN 978-1-338-79726-8

10 9 8 7 6 5 4 3 2 1   23 24 25 26 27

Printed in Italy   183

First edition, April 2023

Book design by Abby Dening

For Ian, Holden, Jimin, and Rango

"Go ask Alice / I think she'll know."

—*Jefferson Airplane*

Table of Contents

(((1)))

A Town Called Poisonberry

I have dreams that Moon and I came here from the past.

In these dreams, my sister, Moon, and I come from a different time period, over two hundred years ago, when we lived in the south before our tribe was removed and forced west by President Andrew Jackson.

And here we are now, in real life, where we live in this desert town in New Mexico called Poisonberry. It's called Poisonberry because there are nasty, bloodred poisonous berries growing all around town. Their shrubs are covered in thorns and grow quickly, sprouting through the cracks in the streets, twisting around houses and buildings, and growing as high as ten feet. Exterminators wearing protective masks and chemical-resistant, baggy clothes have sprayed them, cut them down, destroyed them, but their juice emits a vapor in the air that spreads and makes them multiply even worse.

The weather made it this way. All the rain over the past ten years, even here in the desert, made things grow that have never grown before. My dad says the earth deals with trauma just like people do. The earth remembers how we've treated it for thousands and thousands of years, and now it reacts to the trauma: We have tempestuous seasons, strong rains, high winds, furious storms. The flooding is getting worse. The tornadoes are rolling farther across the country.

Moon and I have lived here in Poisonberry our whole lives. In my dreams, soldiers made us walk until we fell down somewhere in the middle of the desert. In real life, my grandma has told us stories about how our ancestors were removed from their homes. As far back as I can remember, she's always told us stories because we've had to deal with one of the hardest things ever, a tragedy.

When Moon and I were little, our mom disappeared.

Native women go missing all over the country. Nobody seems to be doing much about it. In my mom's case, the sheriff and the police have given up trying to find her. But it's not just her. My friend Sheila has an aunt who is missing. A few other Native kids at my school have relatives who are missing. It's been going on way too long.

I wish I had memories of my mom, but I was just a baby when she vanished. Moon vaguely remembers sitting on her lap, being rocked, listening to her hum. My dad doesn't like to talk about it too much, because it's so painful, but once, he told us that she read and sang to us every night. I wish I remembered that. My memories, instead, involve our dad crying in the house, on their anniversary or on holidays. Our grandma still cries sometimes, too.

So the way it all happened, our mom disappeared and nobody could find her. She was in class at nursing school and didn't come home. Two days after she disappeared, her car was found a few miles away, and she wasn't inside it.

We don't really understand what happened. I wanted my dreams to be true so I could have the power to step through time. I wanted to go back to the past and see her and tell her to stay home from class that night.

It's hard to understand sadness, and how someone can just disappear.

In my dreams, our mom and dad came from the past as well. We live together with our Cherokee ancestors. We are all together, the four of us, and we're happy.

A teacher once told me I daydream a lot and create pretend scenarios in my mind, which is fine, but the teacher thought I couldn't tell the difference between what was real and what wasn't. I know the difference. I know life is life and history is history. But still, I can't help but think of what my life would have been like, back in history. My Cherokee ancestors spent their days hunting for food, skinning deer or elk, and cooking it. They ate under the night sky and listened to elders tell stories or sing. Then everything changed when President Jackson ordered his soldiers to remove the Cherokees from their land, west to Oklahoma, where generations later my mom and dad grew up.

I wish I could go back to the past and fight those soldiers or find a way to trick them. I sometimes pretend I've time-traveled from two hundred years ago and I'm living in this strange world. Once, across the street from the mall, I walked up to the drive-through window of a fast-food restaurant and tried to order a cheeseburger. The guy working there stuck his head out the window and said, "Ya gotta come inside to order on foot." He wore a rumpled paper hat and his eyeglasses were at an angle. I could see the sweat glistening on his forehead.

"I need lunch," I told him. "You cook meat?"

"What are you talking about?" he whined.

Cars were honking at me. I turned and stared at them, a line of automobiles. A man got out of his car and put his hands on his hips.

"Ya gotta come inside to order," the hat guy kept saying from the window. "This lane is for cars."

Another time, at a parade downtown, when I pretended to be from the past, there was a white man dressed as an Indian Chief mascot walking by. I mean, he was wearing a headdress and everything, which is disrespectful to Native culture. I picked up the first thing I could find—a rock about the size of a baseball—and charged him, hitting him in the arm with the rock until the guy got really mad and started yelling at me and pushing me away.

Not long after that, my dad took me to a behavior

specialist, and it turns out I'm introverted and daydreamy and sad a lot, and it can be hard for me to look people directly in the eyes when they talk to me. I like to do things most other kids don't care about, like making long lists of my favorite songs or movies or sitting in my room and talking to my poster of Michael Jordan.

The behavior specialist prescribed a type of medication that I take every day and said I can ask for extra time to do homework and extra test time if I need it. I guess the medication helps me feel better, but I don't really know because it's hard for me to remember what I was like before. It turns out there are lots of kids like me, but I don't know any of them—at least not at Yona Middle School.

My therapist, Kari, says I have anxiety, which can make school and life harder in many ways. She says everyone has anxiety at some point in their lives and it's nothing to be ashamed of. I have trouble making friends, although I have a few good friends at school who don't tease me. I also miss my mom a lot, and I tell Kari about that, too. Kari's nice about it, but that doesn't stop me from wishing it was my mom I was talking to, not her.

Moon has a much easier time than I do at school and around other kids. My grandma says the day after our mom disappeared, Moon stayed in her room all day and wouldn't come out. She never even talked that day. Dad kept banging on the door for her to unlock it and let him in, but she wouldn't. He had to go outside around to the window and force it open, only to find her hiding under her bed with her stuffed animals.

Our dad has never been good about talking about our mom being gone. He's not too good at talking to us about anything serious, to be honest. He means well; he just has a hard time expressing his feelings. He doesn't think I notice this, but I do.

According to my grandma, this wasn't always the case. "It's normal to be afraid and sad," my dad told Moon in a soft voice once he got into her room that first night, as she crawled from underneath the bed. "We're all sad about your mom being gone. I want her to come back, too. We have to learn to accept what we are given in this world."

Unsure of what to say next, he hugged her and left the room.

Weeks passed without a trace of our mom. Months passed, and then a year. *We all became numb from crying*, Grandma told me later. I think you can only cry so much before your body gives up and you feel like all you can do is sleep. I don't like to think about our mom dying, or being kidnapped, but here we are, still without her. Here we are, *ten whole years* after our mom disappeared, still trying to figure out where she is.

As I said, the police gave up on the case a long time ago, which makes me mad.

My history teacher says there are thousands of Native women who go missing every year. Where do they go? Some live, some die, but Moon and I don't want to lose hope. We wonder whether she's alive or dead even though our dad gave up his hope when the police considered the case cold.

I haven't tried to talk to Dad about it in a long time. The last time I tried, I saw the tears gather in his eyes.

"I don't want to talk about it," he said.

Still, he must wonder, too.

I wonder all the time.

(((2)))

ANXIETY

I'm in sixth grade, and Moon is in eighth. That doesn't sound like much, two years apart, but in middle school it's a huge difference. There are some boys in eighth grade who can shave. I've seen guys taller than my dad. There's even one guy who flunked a couple of years and has his driver's license. He pulls into the school parking lot in his low-slung Oldsmobile, windows down and cranking AC/DC. I swear, the guy might be twenty. He's terrifying. Meanwhile, most of us sixth-grade boys are still trying not to let our voices crack.

Moon doesn't acknowledge me much at school. Even though we're close, at school I'm still just a sixth grader.

Moon and I have been seeing Kari for a few years. At first, we talked to her once a week, but now it's every other week. Kari talks to each of us alone, not together. I like her. *Anxiety* is a word I learned from her. You don't have to have a huge mental health issue to see a therapist. Anyone who is feeling sad or afraid can talk to a therapist. Kari is interested in listening to me, I can tell. She isn't pretending to listen the way a lot of adults do. She actually listens, and asks me questions about what I like, how school is going—those sorts of things. One of the first times I talked to her, she told me to visualize my anxiety.

"Think of it as an animal outside of your body," she said. "Look. What do you see?"

I pictured a coyote, because my grandma used to tell me stories about coyotes, plus I like coyotes.

"That coyote is your anxiety," Kari said. "Whenever you start feeling worried, picture the coyote and then talk to it. Look at it and let it know you welcome it. You should know it won't hurt you. Your anxiety is your friend, not something to be afraid of. Do you understand?"

I nodded. I told her I understood, but I didn't, and I was still hurting.

When you have ANXIETY, every thought can lead to a catastrophe. For example, here are some other thoughts that came from my ANXIETY:

All the other kids will think I'm dumb.

The teachers won't like me.

A teacher will call on me for an answer I won't know.

People will laugh at me.

Someone will beat me up or say something to embarrass me in front of everyone.

I might get sick and throw up in the hallway in front of everyone.

Or on the bus. Or in the classroom.

I really did throw up in the classroom once. Right in the middle of music class. It came out of nowhere. We were all standing and singing and mumbling while old Mrs. Vodka played the piano—then suddenly, I leaned forward and hurled. The class fell silent. Andre Malone, standing next to me, fell back into his chair, laughing.

"Go to the restroom," Mrs. Vodka told me. She was an old woman with blue hair and glasses. I remember her look of horror and disgust. As I hurried out of the room, I heard her telling the class in her gravelly voice, "It's fine. We all throw up, kids. Even my husband threw up on our wedding night, fifty years ago. Now someone go fetch the janitor."

I ran all the way down the hall to the bathroom.

Standing there over the sink, all sorts of thoughts raced in my mind: *My life is over. Everyone will now know me as the boy who threw up in class. From this day forward I shall be known as Barf Boy. I'll have to transfer schools or maybe even countries. Maybe I could move to Paris or Spain or Tokyo. Hawaii! Anywhere but here.*

I pictured the headline on the front page of the school paper:

Ziggy Echota Vomits in Music Class
The Vomit Will Haunt Him the Rest of His Life

The good news is that it wasn't nearly as disastrous as I'd expected. In fact, nobody even talked about it, as far as I knew. Even Andre Malone never brought it up again. But that's what

ANXIETY does to you. Catastrophic thoughts race through my mind, and all I ever want to do is stay in my bedroom.

When you start feeling that afraid of everything, it's hard to enjoy anything.

Luckily, at home, my anxiety isn't so bad. It also eases up when I'm playing basketball. Basketball is my favorite sport. Sometimes, Moon and I play basketball in the driveway. I'm not on the team at school because I'm not good enough. The coach lets me be manager, which means I get to assist him with keeping track of statistics and get water and towels for the players. Everyone on the team likes me. I have an OKC Thunder basketball and also posters of Michael Jordan and Kevin Durant in my bedroom. I play basketball on the plastic goal in my room way better than I do in the driveway, but when Moon and I play outside, she helps me a lot. She played until sixth grade, when she became a cheerleader. She's way better than me at a lot of things. I love her a lot. Every now and then I fart on her, and she wrestles me and pins me down.

"You're gross!" she says.

Some nights we lie in the backyard, gaze up at the stars, and wonder where our mom is. Even after all this time, while I know Moon and our dad have given up hope, I still bring up the possibility that she's alive.

"I wonder what Mom's doing right now," I say.

"She's probably helping someone," Moon says.

I think about that. "You think it's possible Mom returned

to the past? And if so, why would she return there without us or Dad?"

"You can't go back to the past," Moon says. "Nobody can go back and change things."

"I bet Mom could."

"Well," Moon says, "if she went to the past, she's needed there. Someone needs her help."

"She wouldn't abandon us."

"Mom loved helping people. She was in school to be a nurse. If it was possible to go back to the past, she would go back and help sick people."

"You're saying she'll come back?"

"No," she says, "I'm not saying that. I'm saying she liked helping people."

I consider this. Whenever I need to think, I have to pace around, so I get up and walk over to the wooden fence in the back of our yard, where a long vine of berries twists over the fence and spills into our yard. I take a handful of berries, eat a few, then walk back over to Moon and sit back down.

"Yum," she says, taking a few from my hand.

We can eat the poisonous berries all the time without getting sick or dying. We've become sort of oddballs around here, as if we've developed an immunity most people don't have. When we were little, our dad caught Moon eating the berries in our backyard. He ran outside and forced the berries out of her hands and mouth until he and she had red juice smeared all over their hands.

But it didn't poison Moon. It didn't even make her sick.

Dad rushed her to the emergency room, and it turned out she was fine. He was shocked. "Are you sure?" Dad said to Dr. Woolfe. "She ate a bunch of them. Maybe they were a different kind of berry?"

"There are no other berries in this town," Dr. Woolfe said.

To be safe, he sent Moon's blood tests to Dr. Gray in Ruidoso, who sent them to Dr. Poole in Albuquerque, who sent them to Dr. Speer in Santa Fe, who sent them back to Dr. Woolfe in Poisonberry with all their test results:

NORMAL

Normal? I guess it's part of what makes us so unique and not of this world. For a while I thought we were ghosts or aliens.

"What are you thinking about?" Moon asks me, taking another berry from my hand.

"I'm thinking about Mom going back to the past, two hundred years ago. Maybe just before the Trail of Tears happened."

"I bet if Mom lived back then, she would've helped someone on the Trail who was sick or dying."

Moon is so much smarter than I am. She's probably the smartest person I know—even smarter than our dad. We take care of each other. Dad works a lot, and we cook dinners and do laundry. Moon understands things I don't, about love and forgiveness, like when someone at school makes me mad, she's always telling me how they might have it worse at home, and it all makes sense.

Moon wipes her hands on her jeans and says, "We better head inside."

When I was eight, I was so fascinated by traveling back to the past, I actually tried going back once. I roamed off into the woods and got lost. Luckily, a neighbor found me before it got dark, but I remember being afraid. I didn't know what I was looking for. I was just calling out for our mom.

"Look," Moon says, pointing up at the sky. "See those stars? What do you think?"

I look up and see the stars and wonder what it must be like to fall into all that space like an astronaut, swimming around in the dark that goes on forever. "In my dreams about Mom," I say, "I can hear her voice coming from somewhere in the sky."

Moon is still looking up, as if searching for something. "Yeah. Dad says Mom was always out exploring things, looking for secret caves out in the desert. Isn't that cool?"

"A secret cave," I say. "That's it! Maybe there's a secret cave out in the desert. Maybe there's a clue out there that would help us find out where she is."

Moon smiles, but she doesn't seem excited about it.

I want to find it, though. After ten years, this world is still not the same without our mom.

"There probably aren't any clues out there or the police would've found them," Moon says.

"Maybe we just need to find the right secret cave."

"Good luck, Ziggy."

"I'm serious," I insist.

"Remember what Dad told us? People go missing all the time, especially kids and women. They usually don't come back, and the police never find out anything about what happened to them. It's terrible but it's just the way it is."

We both fall silent for a moment. Then Moon speaks up. "Well, ask that girl Alice who's in your grade. She's interested in history just like you are. She might know something about caves around here."

"Weird Alice?" I say. "I can't talk to her. She's always staring at me."

Moon shakes her head. "Don't be so afraid of everything, Ziggy. She's a person. You just go up and talk to her in the hall or at lunch."

I've heard all kinds of horrible stories about Weird Alice. Like she sleeps in a coffin in her basement. That she has a pet snake that hisses and spits. That she claims she has seen Cherokee Nunnehi spirits outside of town.

"I don't know," I say.

"Remember she's Cherokee, too," Moon reminds me. "She doesn't hate you. You *have* to talk to her."

"Fine, I'll do it," I say . . . but I'm not feeling good about it.

(((3)))

The Weirdos

I can't stop thinking about the secret cave.

I imagine it hidden out in the desert, buried in a hill somewhere, covered by sand and rock. And the first windstorm of the year, sweeping sand and clumps of desert grass tumbling into the hill, covering the cave's opening. The winds blowing down from the mountain and swirling the dirt enough to keep the hikers away while clouds of sand rise and send birds screaming into a gray sky.

The desert holds all kinds of mysteries. At night, as we sit outside on the porch, we can hear the distant cries of animals, the humming of insects, the gusts of winds. My dad says my mom was fascinated by the mysteries, always hiking and exploring. There are tiny blue lizards crawling around, rattlesnakes slithering underneath rocks. I imagine the owls and the hawks sweeping down to the land. Do all the birds and animals come out at night when the desert is at its darkest? Do they join together and communicate?

If I find the cave, I'll look for drawings on the walls, or secret writings, anything that will give me clues to where my mom is. I'll learn the languages of the animals, the poisonous black snakes and the rattlesnakes and the big mosquitoes. They'll help me find my mom no matter how long it takes. For days, weeks, even months, we will search the cave for hidden tunnels and passageways that lead us underground or through time. I'll eat green berries and red berries and fruit the animals bring me. I'll drink fresh water from cool streams deep underground. Soon we will turn every winding passageway, cross every stream, and find our way to the secret place where my mom will be, and it will be beautiful, and she will hug me and welcome me to stay with her forever in this magical place full of colorful trees and mountains and crystal-blue waters.

Doesn't that sound great?

In the meantime, though, I have to go to school. Yona Middle School is about a ten-minute drive from our house, but most of the time it takes longer to get there because you have to cross the railroad tracks, and in the mornings around eight, there's always a train holding up traffic.

"Stupid train," our dad says in the pickup. I'm sitting in the back seat and Moon is up front. The pickup is a battered old Ford with a broken air conditioner, but as my dad always tells us, "It gets us from here to there." Now Dad hits the heel of his hand against the steering wheel in frustration, and I know something else must be bothering him. For one thing, he usually turns on the radio and talks when he drives us to school, but today he doesn't turn on the radio or talk much at all.

I know not to say anything. Moon, however, is braver than I am. She leans over and tries to playfully poke him in the ribs.

"Hey, Grumpy," she says. "Didn't get your coffee this morning?"

The train roars by in front of us.

"It's nothing," Dad tells her, shaking his head. "Look at your phone or something."

Moon looks back at me, and I shrug.

"I don't believe you," she tells him. "You can't hide it from us. Something's the matter. You're never so quiet."

"Nothing, nothing," he says.

"Don't believe you. Cough it up or else."

"Moon . . ."

"You can't fool me. Nope."

I'm not sure why Moon keeps pressing him. I would never do that, out of fear he would yell at me. But he never yells at Moon. Maybe he respects her for challenging him. Maybe he wishes I would talk to him more.

"It's your grandma," he says. "She's coming to stay with us again for a few days because they're kicking her out of her retirement village."

"They're kicking her out? Why?"

He shakes his head, disappointed. "Smoking cigarettes. She won't stop smoking. She ignores the rules. She leaves when she's not supposed to, disappearing from time to time."

"Where does she go?"

"She says she has to ride around the desert," he says. "So she has to come stay with us for a while."

"Ride around the desert?" I say.

Moon looks back at me, and I know what she's thinking. The last two times our grandma came to visit us were disasters. First, there was a year or so ago when she got caught stealing a can of snuff from a local smoke shop she had snuck off to. She couldn't drive Dad's truck, so she walked everywhere, usually early in the mornings when we were asleep. Then last summer she went for a walk and picked some of the poisonous berries and ended up breaking out in hives so badly we had to rush her to the emergency room so she could get a shot in her butt. Unfortunately, I was in the room with her and Dad to witness it. Trust me on this: The last person you ever want to see get a shot in the butt is your grandma. I've never told anyone about it.

"How long does she have to stay?" I ask.

"I don't know," Dad replies. "I guess until we can find someplace else for her to live."

"Where will she sleep? On the floor?"

He looks at me in the rearview mirror. "She'll sleep in your room. You can sleep on the fold-out couch."

"My room?" I say. "Why my room? Can't she sleep on the couch or in the tub or something?

"She's almost seventy years old, Ziggy. She can't sleep in a tub."

"It's not fair," I tell him.

"Last time Moon shared a room with her. You'll take the couch. I'll pick you up right after school to help her move her things."

"What about Moon?"

Moon turns her head, and I can tell she's trying not to laugh. "I have cheerleading practice," she says. "But I'm sure you can handle it."

Our grandma is Cherokee, my mom's mom. It's hard for her to find a place to stay that's close enough to where we live so that my dad can help out when he needs to because she doesn't have any other family. I don't want to think about her taking over the house. And worse, it's depressing because whenever she's around, it makes me miss my mom even more. My day is starting out miserably.

Our dad rubs his hand over his face and sighs. I can tell he's stressed about it. The train finally passes and the gate lifts so we can move forward and cross the railroad tracks.

As we pull into the parking lot at school, I see my friends Corso and Bojack-Runt standing by the flagpole. Dad stops the car and tells us to study hard and be good. We get out and Moon hurries over to her circle of friends.

"Listen to your teachers," Dad calls from the window, then drives off.

At Yona Middle School, the boys usually stand on one side of the yard and the girls on the other. However, Corso and Bojack-Runt always stand by the flagpole in the middle, which means I stand there with them because they're my best friends. Bojack-Runt says it's safer there by the flagpole because we're more visible to the teachers in case anyone decides to mess with us. He's the smallest of anyone in our class, which is how he earned the name Bojack-Runt.

"You got mustard on your shirt," Corso says as I approach.

I see the stain in the middle of my shirt. "It's jelly from my toast. Crap, it looks terrible."

Corso leans in and touches it. "Looks like mustard. Feels like mustard."

"It's not mustard—stop saying that." I spit in my hand and rub my shirt to try to get the stain out, but it only makes it worse. When I look up, Sheila and Vicious Sid are approaching us.

"Hey," Sheila says, "have you guys thought of a name for the band yet?"

"Hang on just a second," Bojack-Runt says. He unclips his briefcase and takes out a pencil and a notebook. "I'll jot the ideas down. Go."

"Lizard Tongue," Corso says.

Sheila laughs.

"What's so funny? I was thinking it sounded cool, like the Boomtown Rats."

"Well, Lizard Tongue isn't good. It's terrible."

"Fine. Wolf Tongue? Pig Tongue?"

"Gah! Stop with the tongues."

"Planet Head Gash? Tiger Spit?"

"No, gah!"

Here's the story: Corso's the only white person in our group. The rest of us are Native. There aren't many Natives at Yona Middle School, so we tend to stick together and watch out for each other as much as we can. Sheila is Corso's girlfriend. She's the drummer and singer in their band. Corso plays guitar and Vicious Sid plays bass. We call him Vicious Sid because he's so shy and timid—the last thing he would ever be is vicious. He rarely talks, preferring to express himself through his guitar playing.

Bojack-Runt is the manager of the band, which is why he's constantly writing ideas down and trying to get them gigs at parties or events. So far they haven't played anywhere except in Corso's garage.

"I came up with a few ideas," Bojack-Runt says, flipping through his notebook. "Here's one. How about the Zits?"

"No!" Sheila and Corso both say at the same time.

"Big Hairy Beards?"

"None of us have beards," Corso says. "Also—gross."

"How about the Basketballers," I suggest.

They all look at each other, then at me, which clearly means no.

Bojack-Runt adjusts his glasses. "Karma and the Detectives? It's as random as Question Mark and the Mysterians, who were a real band. My dad has their album at home."

"We don't care," Corso replies. "How about Sheila Take a Bow?"

"No," Sheila says, closing her eyes in frustration.

Vicious Sid sits cross-legged right there beside us and pulls his black sweater over his head, always his way of showing he's frustrated.

"You're stressing out Sid," I tell them.

"The name has to be a perfect marriage of irony and rebellion," Bojack-Runt says. "Think of Talking Heads. Or the Replacements. Or Garbage."

We all stare at Bojack-Runt.

The first-period bell rings, and I see a group of sixth-grade girls heading toward the front doors, but I can't find Alice anywhere. Not at lunch in the cafeteria, not in the halls during the day. Besides drawing airplanes or dogs, I spend much of the day staring out the window at school. It's one of my favorite things to do, gaze outside and daydream. I find shapes in the wild branches of trees, red berries in a blue sky. My mother's face in the clouds.

When I walk into my last-period math class, it's such a relief to see Alice that I actually let out "YES!" the moment I spot her sitting at her desk. Everyone laughs, and Mr. Shankley sighs.

"Ziggy," he says, "stop lollygagging and go sit down."

The bell rings. I sit at my desk and look over at Alice, but she won't look at me. Guys make fun of her for dyeing her hair, which is horrible and mean, but it doesn't seem to bother her. One time, this guy named Matt was sitting right beside her, and he cupped his hands like a megaphone and asked her in a loud voice if she was an alien. But it didn't embarrass her. She turned and flipped him off right there in front of the whole class, which made everyone cheer for her. The teacher saw it all and sent Matt to the office and let Alice stay. Sometimes that group of bullies will make fun of the way she occasionally talks in Cherokee. She's tough, though. When we were in fifth grade, I once saw her beat up a seventh-grade boy at the bus stop, and ever since then I've been afraid of her. This is why I'm nervous to talk to her about secret caves.

In class, Mr. Shankley bites from an apple as he takes roll. "Frye? Anyone seen Frye today? Or what about Tommy?"

We all look around.

"There's no one named Frye in this class," a girl says. "And Tommy is getting his tonsils out."

Mr. Shankley sighs over the wastebasket. His posture is bad, like he's defeated. As he turns and writes out math problems on the whiteboard, I rip a sheet of paper from my notebook and write Alice a note:

> Siyo, Alice!
> I want to ask u something very, very important (it is not a bad thing). Can u meet me after class? (outside or in the hall is fine!)
>   Signed, Ziggy

She's sitting two rows over from me, so I fold the note and lean over to Adam Mandt, who is hunched forward, drawing what looks like two gigantic ducks. When he sees the note in my hand, he takes it and unfolds it.

"Pass it to Alice," I whisper.

"Why?" he whispers back.

"Shhh. Pass it on."

"I'm going to read it. Every word!"

"No—pass it, please!"

Adam points at the note, making a face like he's screaming. People turn around and look at us, and I realize Mr. Shankley has stopped writing at the board and is watching us, too. The room is silent.

"Gentlemen," Mr. Shankley says, slumped forward. "Is there a problem? Is that a *note*?"

Adam folds it back and I look around, pretending I don't know what he's talking about.

"Ziggy," Mr. Shankley says, running a hand over his face. "Pass it forward, Adam."

Adam Mandt passes it forward to Chrissie Hind, who hands it to Brian Fairey, who hands it to Robert Smith, who hands it to Mr. Shankley.

"Frankly," says Mr. Shankley, "since you all know my class rules, I'm going to have to read this aloud."

My heart races, and I want to crawl out of the window or disappear. Mr. Shankley then reads the note aloud, which makes everyone laugh, including Adam.

Robert Smith, who dresses in black every day and wears eyeliner, says, "Tomorrow's Friday, and Ziggy's in love."

Everybody laughs again.

My ANXIETY kicks in and I start drawing circles on my

paper—long circles, small circles, squiggly lines. I have to keep drawing wild, circular designs and not look at anyone.

"Pipe down," Mr. Shankley says, running his hand over his balding head. "No more shenanigans, guys. Get back to work."

I'm too embarrassed to glance over at Alice, even though it feels like she's looking at me. I keep my head down and do my work for the rest of the class until the bell finally rings.

Slowly, I stuff my folder into my backpack and wait for everyone to leave the classroom. When I look up, I notice Alice is already gone. In the front of the room, Mr. Shankley is waiting for me with the note.

"Ziggy," he says wearily, and I see the disappointment in his face. That look makes me feel worse. "You have to learn to concentrate. Stay focused. We've talked about this before."

I nod, look down at the floor.

"Have a good day," he says.

On the way to my locker I try to find Corso, but he's already gone. Down the hall I see Bojack-Runt headed for the door, so I call out to him.

He turns and looks to me. "Hey, Ed, I'm in a hurry."

Bojack-Runt has called me Ed since the first grade. His family moved here when we were in first grade, and for whatever reason he thought my name was Ed for about a week until we became friends. Now he still calls me Ed. Neither of us thinks anything about it anymore.

"I'm late for band practice at Corso's," he goes on. "If I'm late, Corso will fire me."

I hurry toward him with my backpack. "He can't fire you. He's not in charge of the band."

Bojack-Runt adjusts his glasses and looks confused.

"You're the manager," I tell him, following him toward the door. "You keep track of all the contacts. You make all the phone calls for gigs. Nobody else wants to do that. So he won't fire you. Trust me, I know Corso."

"I have a very busy schedule," he says. "Band practice means work, Ed. Making calls and scheduling gigs. Then it's home for dinner and homework. Trash duty. Reading time. French lessons online, and word games before bed."

We step outside in the sun. "You're taking French lessons?" I ask him.

"Absolutely. I hope to travel someday. I want to be ahead of the game. My Spanish is coming along, so I want to get ahead in French and possibly take German or Japanese in high school."

"Are you for real?"

"Ed, this is serious business. The time is now. We can't lollygag around, like Mr. Shankley is always saying. Prepare now for a bright future."

"You sound like a bad commercial."

"I'm hoping to get into a good college, Ed. There aren't enough of us Cherokees out there in the business world."

Bojack-Runt really does take his work seriously. He takes *everything* seriously, and sometimes I wonder if he ever allows himself to have fun. Other than playing word games before bed.

"You seem tense," he continues. "Why don't you go get

yourself a good solid massage? My dad goes to a massage ther-apist somewhere near the bowling alley, and he says it does wonders for his back and neck and posture."

I stop walking because I see Alice standing by the flagpole, watching us. She comes over and Bojack-Runt takes a step back.

"You looking for trouble, Runt?" she says to him. Then she shows him her fist.

"No." He swallows. "Actually, I need to go to band practice. I'll see you there, Ed?"

"Sure," I tell him, and he scampers away.

Alice glares at me, trying not to laugh.

"I—I wanted to ask you a question," I sputter, the ANXIETY getting even louder.

"You don't have to write me notes," she says. "You can just talk to me."

"Yeah, sorry about that."

"Don't apologize, Ziggy. You apologize all the time. I hear you apologizing in the hallways."

"Sorry."

"See what I mean?"

I'm not sure whether Alice is angry or what. She continues to stare at me.

"My sister and I were talking last night," I say, "and she told me you know a lot about the history around here. About the desert, and caves, and that sort of stuff."

I avoid her eyes and see her hearing aid in her ear. It's flesh colored and hard to tell it's even there.

She takes her sunglasses out of her backpack and puts them on.

"Yeah?" she says. "What about it? What do you want to know?"

"I mean," I say, finding it hard to articulate what I want to ask her, "Moon and I were talking about our mom last night."

"Your mom? What about her?"

"You probably know she's been missing since I was a baby. She liked to explore the desert and find rocks, caves, secret places, those sorts of things. And we were hoping there was a cave or something we could find that would help us track her down."

"A cave?"

"Maybe? Or something, anything really, to help us find our mom. The police gave up a long time ago."

"I know there are some caves out in the desert," she says. "But I'm not sure you'll find anything there."

I wonder whether she's made the whole thing up about being a cave expert, and just tells people about it for attention or something, but I have to tell her more. It's too important. An image of my mother flashes in my mind, so I blurt it out:

"I mean, look, I know it's a long shot. A very, very long shot. But it's possible she went into those caves. And maybe there's something there that can help me find her." I don't tell her about the thing in the back of my mind, about my dreams of her traveling back in time to our home, where we come from. For some reason, I find myself on the verge of feeling my eyes tear up, and I turn away.

Alice doesn't say anything. I look at my feet, at the ground, then I kneel and retie my shoelaces.

"I'm sorry about your mom," Alice says. "The same thing happened to my older sister, Andrea. She disappeared a hundred years ago. I don't tell many people."

"A hundred years ago?"

"I'm exaggerating."

"Oh."

"Well, anyway, I can show you the caves, but you have to keep it a secret. The Nunnehi live there, so we have to respect their privacy."

I stand back up and look at her. "Really?"

"Yeah, but you can't tell anyone, okay?"

When I was little, my grandma told me stories about how the Cherokee Nunnehi lived in underground tunnels and traveled around to help our ancestors when called upon. They were spirits, mostly invisible, but they could appear in human form if they wanted. They told stories. Our ancestors walked the Trail and gained courage with the help of the Nunnehi.

"Were they dangerous?" I asked my grandma.

"If they needed to be," she answered.

"Did they fight the soldiers?"

"Mostly they helped other Cherokees," she said. "But they found joy in being tricksters, like turning themselves into coyotes or hawks. They chased the soldiers and frightened them. But they were entirely themselves. Also, they're still around, and they love music, which is why you can still sometimes hear music coming from the desert at night."

I imagined all the people who were sick and dying along the Trail. I'd always thought of only sad images, but then I started picturing the hawks flying down on the soldiers, or dogs showing their teeth and growling at them, and I liked thinking about that.

"All right," I say to Alice. "Hey, I can show you something secretive, too, if you want. It has to do with my friend Corso. Nobody other than me knows except his band: Bojack-Runt, Vicious Sid, and Sheila. You want to go see it? You won't believe it! He lives just a few blocks away."

Alice looks around for a moment. "The bus is leaving. How will you get home?"

"Oh, I'll just call my dad from Corso's," I say, and we head down the sidewalk in the direction of Corso's house. We walk past berries that have fallen from the trees, and I make sure to help Alice so she doesn't step on one.

(((4)))

The Magic Guitar

Corso lives in a yellow house with an attached garage where the band practices every day after school. They practice before Corso's parents get home from work; that way they can play as loud as they want. I don't go over there very often because I can't handle the noise. I mean, Sheila has a nice voice—she's in the school choir and in school musicals where she sings solos and usually steals the show. So it isn't her that makes the band sound so lousy. It's Corso's and Vicious Sid's guitar playing. Seriously, it's so loud I can't tell if they're always out of tune, or out of rhythm, or both.

As soon as Alice and I arrive and step into the garage, we hear the shrill of Corso's electric guitar and the *thawmp-thawmp-thawmp* of Sid's bass. I have to cover my ears. The garage is full of posters of rock bands and old cars. There's a dirty lawn mower and cans of paint stacked in the corner, and the place looks ragged with empty Coke cans and candy wrappers scattered around.

Sheila sees us and stops playing the drums, but Corso and Sid keep going, their eyes closed, heads rocking to the sound of their own music.

"Hey!" Sheila says.

Sid opens his eyes, sees us, and stops playing. He reaches over and taps Corso on the shoulder to get him to stop.

Corso opens his eyes and takes his hands off his guitar. "Oh, hey," he says.

Nobody knows what to say when they see Alice with me. I'm not sure whether Sheila and Alice get along, to be honest, but Sheila waves from her drums and says, "Hey, Alice."

Alice waves back.

"What are you guys doing?" Corso asks.

"I thought I'd bring Alice to see the magic guitar," I explain, suddenly nervous that Corso won't be all right with this plan. What have I gotten myself into?

Corso glances at Alice, then back at me. "Magic guitar?"

"Yeah," I say. "I told her about it. I hope that's okay. Is it okay?"

Corso looks confused.

I point to the guitar. "How it *glows*?"

"Oh," he says. "Well, that's not really magic." He looks at Alice. "The guitar has a special paint that makes it glow in the dark. That's what Ziggy is talking about, if you want to see it."

"We want to see it," I say.

Corso closes the garage door, then hits the light switch so

the room falls completely dark. We see his guitar glow purple in the dark.

He plays a few guitar licks.

"Look," I say to Alice, nudging her. "Isn't it cool how it glows?"

Corso flips the lights back on and I applaud, but everyone is staring at me. Alice has her arms crossed, disappointed.

"What?" I say to everyone.

"This is what you wanted to show me?" Alice says. "A glow-in-the-dark guitar? Seriously?"

"He's so amazed by it," Sheila tells her. "You'd think he's never seen anything glow in the dark before."

"The purple is beautiful in the dark," I tell them. "Why is that so weird?"

"Nobody said it was weird," Sheila says. "We all love you, Ziggy."

I know they love me. They're my friends, and they've never made fun of me about how different I am. I never have to explain anything to them, which makes me feel good.

But I'm disappointed about the purple glow on the guitar because Alice is disappointed. I wanted her to love it as much as I do. "Where I come from," I tell them, "we don't have glow-in-the-dark things. There aren't even electric guitars. Not even electricity."

"We know, we know," Corso says.

Vicious Sid sets his bass guitar on its stand and comes over to me and puts his arm around me. It's his way of telling me he cares about how I'm feeling.

He holds his fist out to me. I give him a fist bump and he goes back to his guitar.

Suddenly the garage door opens, and Bojack-Runt is standing there with his big smile, talking on his cell phone. He hangs up and gives us a thumbs-up.

"You won't believe it," he says. "I booked a gig for the band this Saturday! It'll be downtown. I just talked to Mayor Simpleton, and he's excited about it."

Everyone is happy, except maybe Alice. She's staring at the posters on Corso's wall of the famous guitar players. I go over to her and ask if she's mad. I'm worried she won't show me the cave.

She turns to me. "Mad at what?"

"At me."

"For what? Bringing me here? No, not at all, Ziggy."

"Are you sure?"

Corso interrupts us and calls out, "Hey, Alice, do you have a band name for us?"

She looks at everyone. "A band name? You guys can't come up with anything?"

"Nothing good," Sheila tells her.

Bojack-Runt speaks up. "I have a few more ideas if anyone wants to hear them."

"No!" everyone says at the same time.

Sheila's back at her drums and tells everyone they're going to practice their song "I Love You, Jack White!"

She counts off the beat, tapping her drumsticks together, and the band starts playing. I have to cover my ears. Corso's guitar is too loud for me, so I step outside the garage. I walk over to the chain-link fence where it's quieter.

I hear Sheila yell from the garage: "Jack White, Jack White! I love you, Jack White!"

There's a small dog in the next yard, a black-and-brown Lab mix. The dog hurries over to me and sticks its nose through the fence. I kneel and scratch under its chin, let it lick my hand. It's a sweet dog.

Moon and I had a dog once, a few years after our mom disappeared. My dad got her from the shelter to cheer us up. Her name was Pepper. She was a sweet mutt who loved playing tug-of-war with a blanket or towel, and she used to sleep on Moon's pillow every night, right beside her head. Sadly, one day we came home from school and Pepper was gone. She'd gotten out of the fence and had run away. She'd been with us for only about a year. Our mother had disappeared and now Pepper was gone, too. So we decided not to get another pet because we all loved that dog so much.

As I'm petting the dog, I hear Alice say my name, so I stand back up and turn to her.

"Are you sure you want to see the cave?" Alice asks me.

"Yeah," I say. "Why do you ask?"

"Well, the Nunnehi play music in their cave most nights. It can get pretty loud sometimes. They can be obstreperous."

I look at her. "Obstreperous?"

"Noisy and out of control," she replies. "Sort of like this band."

"What kind of music do they play?"

"Any kind you want," she says. "They sing and dance. They drum."

"Do they play electric guitars?"

"No, there aren't electric guitars."

"Then I should be fine."

"But the singing and drums can get loud. Are you okay with that?"

I think about it. I try to imagine the Nunnehi and hearing their music. It is daunting but exciting.

Just then my dad's pickup pulls into the driveway. He sticks his head out the window and says, "Ziggy! Why don't you ever check your phone? I've been looking everywhere for you—come on!"

"I gotta go," I tell Alice.

"See you soon, Ziggy," she says.

As I put on my backpack and walk to the pickup, I can still hear Corso's shrieking guitar and Sheila singing, "Jack White! Jack White!"

(((5)))

Grandma Moses

On the drive home from Corso's, I know my dad is angry because he doesn't say anything until we pull into the driveway and he cuts the engine.

"Be nice to your grandma," he tells me. "She's sensitive. When you weren't anywhere to be found after school, I had to bring her here to go look for you. She was worried."

My grandma's name is Moses, like the famous artist. Seriously, it's even on her birth certificate. Moses Annie Calico. When she was young, Grandma Moses won a beauty contest. My dad told me she went off to college somewhere east but then returned before her freshman year ended. Moon says that Grandma realized she needed to return home and help people—I don't really know what that means, but something happened to her that made her drop out of school and come home. That was a long time ago.

Grandma has told us stories about yansa, buffalo, running

from ajila, a great fire that happened when she was little that burned a field and crops. A drought followed, and people were starving and struggling to get food. Swarms of insects swirled around in the air. Then a massive thunderstorm swept across the land, and a plague of frogs arrived. My grandma caught many walosi, frogs, and took care of them, feeding them and then setting them free in the flooded waters. Something changed in her then, she told us. She felt compelled to help people.

"Frogs taught me the value in taking care of things," she told us.

I look out the window at the house. A few birds scatter into the sky. I can already imagine my grandma standing inside with her pipe in her mouth, waiting to hug me for ten minutes without letting go. She smokes a pipe for some reason. She's done it for years, and it's a miracle she's still alive after so many years of smoking. I imagine her standing in there, telling me about her sore spine or feet problems. Blowing her nose and coughing.

"I forgot she was coming," I say.

"You have to remember to write things down," my dad says. "Remember what we talked about with Kari? Writing in your planner and checking it every day. You have a schedule of things to do every day."

I nod, but I can't look at him.

Maybe this is the way it is without a mom. When you lose someone close to you, it's easy to see how much you take them for granted. For example, when I would come home from school, I usually played basketball by myself while Moon was at drama club, and by the time she got home we were all hungry and expected our dad to make supper for us. After work, he took a shower because he worked construction, and he was tired and hungry, and soon Moon said she knew he was too exhausted to cook. We learned to help out as much as we could. Most of the time Moon never asked me to help, she just did things like that on her own, which made me even sadder because it was so much work. How could we manage to survive without our mom?

I already knew how to make soup and sandwiches and bacon in the microwave, so some nights when Moon has a school function or game she has to be at, that's what we have: ham, bacon, and cheese sandwiches and soup. Some nights we get Chinese takeout, or my dad grills chicken while Moon cuts potatoes and carrots and pours a sack of salad into a large bowl. Our grandma taught Moon how to cook spaghetti and boil green beans in a saucepan, and soon enough she got pretty good at cooking it so that my dad appreciated it. I help out by setting the table. We manage, the three of us, to get everything done. Then my grandma fell and broke her hip at her nursing home, and my dad kept worrying about her, so things got a little harder.

For as long as I can remember, I've worried that my dad will die, too, and that Moon and I will end up having to go live in a group home or with a foster family. I know a couple of kids from school who are in group homes because their parents aren't around anymore, so it's scary. I worry that we'll be left by ourselves or have to drop out of school to get a job to pay our rent because we don't have much money. I worry my dad will get sick and lose his job.

I have anxiety, so I worry a lot.

"Just be nice to your grandma," my dad tells me as we get out of the truck. "She wants to talk to you. Be super nice."

"Super nice," I repeat.

I follow my dad into the house, where my grandma is sitting in a rocking chair by the window. Her hair is blue. I've never seen a woman with such blue hair—I imagine my grandma would win the bluest-hair award, if they ever give such an award. Plus she's puffing at her pipe, filling the room with smoke. I must be the only kid in town whose grandma loves tobacco so much she smokes a pipe.

"Oh, my sweet little Ziggy-bear," she says in a cloud. "Come here, boy."

She tries to stand, but my dad hurries over and tells her to stay seated. I set my backpack down and walk over to her, lean in and hug her. She takes my cheeks in her hands and kisses me on the forehead with a cold mouth—something she does whenever she greets me—and I feel her cold fingers on my face, all skin and bone. Why is she so cold all the time? Always cold and smoky. I have to hold my breath.

"I brought you something," she says. "It's in my bag in your bedroom. Go get it and bring it here."

I hurry into my bedroom, where I see her suitcase on the

floor beside her purse. The bag is on the bed, but first I grab my mini basketball and slam-dunk in my basket over my closet door. I shoot a few shots, do a head fake left and drive right to do a windmill dunk. I pretend dribble, spin around, and do an easy layup. This has become a drill of my own, after school and before bed. I look at my posters and give Jordan and Durant a thumbs-up.

Back in the living room, in front of my grandma, I open the bag and find a small brown book. I open it and see my mom's name, written in cursive. As I flip through the pages, I see drawings of trees, houses, clouds. On one page there's a dog chasing a bird. On another, there's a little girl sticking out her tongue.

"It was your mom's sketchbook," Grandma explains. "She loved to draw when she was a little girl. I thought you would like it since you like to draw, too. Look at it when you're feeling sad. It's guaranteed to make you feel better."

I'm not sure what to say. I keep looking at the drawings. There's a little boy with a giant lollipop. There are trees with faces. Houses with faces. They're all smiling.

"Thank you," I tell her, and then I lean into the cloud of smoke and hug her again. Grandma lets out a long moan followed by laughter. She really is losing her mind, I think. Dad is right to be worried about her. Also, she smells like a mixture of tobacco and pee.

After supper that night, I finish my homework at the kitchen table, then help my dad pull out the sofa bed in the living room and put sheets on it. Moon is doing homework in her own room. My grandma has already gone into *my* room and gotten into bed, and it's not even nine.

"Why does she go to bed so early?" I ask.

Dad's sitting in the recliner while I sit on the sofa bed. "She gets tired," he says. "It happens as you get older. Oh, by the way, remember that you don't have your appointment with Kari tomorrow. She's on vacation."

"It's nice to have a week off from her, I guess," I say.

"I thought you liked talking to her?"

"I do, but sometimes there's nothing to say. Or I say the same thing over and over every week."

My dad pulls off his boots and leans back with his eyes closed. He looks sad or worried about something. It's probably me. I want to talk to him about it, but I can't bring myself to say anything. Better to leave him alone, give him his silence and solitude. Better to wait for him to talk to me.

I sit on the sofa bed and play my Nintendo Switch. Soon he gets up and takes his boots with him into his bedroom, and I know I won't see him for the rest of the night. He'll retreat to his room where he'll lie in bed and watch TV until he falls asleep. Some nights I've awoken to voices that frighten me, but they're coming from the TV in his bedroom. I tiptoe in there and turn it off for him.

My grandma is in my room, so I can't play basketball in there. It's killing me not to be able to shoot my baskets before bed. It sounds ridiculous, I know, but doing it makes me feel better. It relieves all my worries. In a way, it feels like it can bring me good luck. Not shooting baskets only makes me want to do it more.

Instead, I try to substitute for the ritual. I shoot an invisible ball into an invisible basket. I spin and do a dunk. I jump, dribble across the room, and do one monster dunk with both hands.

Just then Moon appears in the hall. "What are you doing?"

"Playing hoops," I say.

"Um, there's no hoop or basketball in here? Are you serious?"

"I have to pretend or else I can't sleep. I do it every night in my room but Grandma's in there snoring."

Moon looks at me like I'm ridiculous. "Why don't you just draw or something?"

"One more," I say, and spin around and double-pump a dunk. I realize it looks strange without a basketball or goal, but I feel so much better afterward. I plop down on the sofa bed.

"When Mom appears in my dreams, sometimes she's looking for a little dog," I tell her.

Moon looks concerned. She doesn't say anything. She just stands there looking at me, like she's trying to figure out what to say.

"I don't know what it means," I say. "Probably nothing."

"What kind of dog?" she asks.

I try to think, but I can't remember. "I don't know, but it isn't always a dog. Sometimes it's a rabbit. Sometimes it's a snake or a frog."

"She's looking for animals?"

"Yeah."

"Hmm, I wonder what it means."

"Maybe she's looking for us?" I ask. "Is that what it means?"

"Hmm," she says, thinking. We're both silent a minute. Then Moon says, "Maybe it's her way of telling you to pay attention to animals."

"Huh?"

"To be nice to them. To respect them. Dad once told me that she volunteered at an animal shelter for a while before we were born."

I think about this. It makes sense. Moon is so much smarter than I am that I always agree with her. "I want to be like her," I say. "I want to explore the desert and see if there are any secret caves or anything to find out there. Do you want to come with me?"

"To explore caves in the desert?"

"Yeah. Today I talked to that girl Alice like you suggested, and she says the Nunnehi are out there sometimes. How cool would it be to see one? Can you imagine it? They helped our ancestors."

Moon sits on the edge of the sofa bed and stares at me. "I don't think you should . . ." She hesitates.

"What?" I say.

"I mean . . ." she says. "Well, I don't think there's a secret place to find Mom, Ziggy."

"What are you talking about?"

"I just think we need to try to accept that she's gone, like Dad always tells us."

"Well, we can just explore the area for caves like she did. It sounds fun to me."

Moon looks at me, and in this look I can see she's not interested.

"Do what you want, but I'm going," I tell her. "I'm exploring the desert for caves and anything else I can find."

I put on my headphones and lie back on the sofa bed. Moon heads down the hall to her bedroom.

I guess I'm really going to have to do this on my own.

(((6)))

Yona Middle School

The next morning I wake to my grandma standing over me with her pipe in her mouth. She's the first thing I see when I open my eyes, and it startles me so much I let out a shriek.

"Better get up," she says, tapping my leg.

"Grandma?" I say, because I'm still partly asleep and also because she's staring at me through her big, old-lady glasses. She lights her pipe as I gaze up at her.

"Time for school," she says, blowing smoke. "Your dad and sister are up. Get dressed."

Slightly hunched, she shuffles over to the recliner. I get out of bed and hurry into my bedroom to get dressed and gather my things for school. I remember my conversation with Moon and feel frustrated she doesn't want to go find our mom with me. I decide I'll give her the silent treatment until she can't stand it.

The whole drive to school, even as we sit in the pickup

47

waiting for the train to pass, I don't say anything to her. Our dad turns up the radio and we hear an old, twangy country-and-western song. The singer sounds like an old man yodeling, whining about feeling lovesick. What does *lovesick* even mean? Isn't love supposed to be a good feeling, and does it actually involve feeling sick? I love my family but I don't feel sick. I miss my mom, which I guess is sort of a sick feeling. Maybe lovesickness means just missing someone? Lovesick? What the heck does it mean?

The more I think about things like this, the more confused I feel. I stare out the window as the train roars by and think about how old the guy was when he recorded the song, and how old the train roaring by is, and how old my mom would be if she were still here with us.

I wish we could just go back in time. In fifth grade, I became obsessed with time travel after we read *The Time Machine* by H. G. Wells. For fifth-grade science fair, I made my own time machine, a cardboard box I spray-painted silver and drew on knobs and circuits, but then this kid Brett told everyone it was just a stupid cardboard box and not a time machine at all. He said it right in front of the whole class. I knew it didn't work, but the point was that he couldn't even pretend to imagine it. You build a rocket, it doesn't really go to space. Yet Brett's rocket won second place while my time machine was an honorable mention.

By the time we get to school, the bell has rung and people are crowding toward the front doors. I tell my dad bye and run away before Moon has a chance to say anything to me. It is windy and chilly this morning, but the sun is shining bright, giving me a dizzy sense of my surroundings. Shadows from the trees sprawl across the parking lot, while red and yellow leaves tumble in the wind across the path as I make my way to the front doors.

The day hinges on the odd feeling that the season is changing to fall. Something about the way the weather shifts during the school year feels oogly and melancholy to me every year around this time. Fall is here and winter is coming. Thinking about it makes me sleepy and dazed. That's how the whole day feels, in fact. In class I have trouble staying awake, probably due to not sleeping as well since I was on the couch last night.

"Ed, you look puckered," Bojack-Runt says at lunch.

I glance at him. "Puckered?"

"Yeah. Tired, worn out."

"You mean tuckered?"

He looks confused. We're sitting at our usual table in the corner of the cafeteria. We're usually the first to arrive at our table since we have gym the period before lunch. Our gym teacher, Mr. Jughead, also coaches wrestling and football and lets us leave class two minutes early before the bell rings because the gymnasium is across campus from the cafeteria. His real name is Mr. Clark, but he has a large head and no neck and everyone just calls him Mr. Jughead. His favorite food is beef jerky. He told us he once put his head through a wall in college at a party and walked away unscathed.

"I hate gym class," I say.

"I thought you hated all of Yona Middle School like the rest of us," Bojack-Runt says.

"I do hate Yona Middle School, but I hate gym class even more. Jughead makes us run laps around the football field for no reason. We're not in training."

"It's his way of pretending he has a real job. I'm sure he plans his day out on the drive to work. 'What'll I have the kids do today? Run laps while I read the paper and sip coffee!'"

Vicious Sid, Corso, and Sheila all arrive and set their trays down. "What's up, everyone?" Sheila asks.

"Ed here is feeling extra puckered," Bojack-Runt says.

"Tuckered," I say. "My grandma is staying with us. Plus, she's sleeping in my bed, so I have to take the couch."

"I hate it when my grandparents stay with us," Corso says. "My grandpa hogs the bathroom and the whole house smells like his aftershave lotion. It takes about a week for the smell to go away."

"I like aftershave lotion," Bojack-Runt says. "It's especially useful when I have to attend social functions. There's a dance next week at the Eagle Club. You guys going?"

"I don't like to dance," Corso says.

"Me either," I say.

Vicious Sid shakes his head slowly and retreats under his hood.

"What kind of dance do you do?" Sheila asks.

"Interpretive," Bojack-Runt says. "Depending on the mood

or rhythm of the song. My mom makes me go."

"Interpretive?" I say. "Is that a real style of dance, like playing air guitar?"

"Of course, Ed. Think about it. It's more to do with feeling the lyrics and overall tone of the music. Expressing it all with your full body."

Corso looks amazed, mouth agape.

I notice Alice carrying her tray to a table nearby. I call out to her, but she doesn't respond.

"She didn't hear you," Sheila says. "I'll go get her."

"No, wait—I'll do it." I get up in such a hurry my shoelace snags under the chair and I trip and fall, which causes a riot of laughter all around the cafeteria. I'm too embarrassed to do anything but lie there a minute before I go back to my seat. My ANXIETY is kicking in!

"That was embarrassing," I say. "Oh no."

"Maybe nobody saw," Corso says. "It's possible, right?"

"I heard laughter," I tell him. "Oh no. Oh no."

"Take it easy, Ed," Bojack-Runt says. "Don't let your anxiety get the best of you."

I take a pencil and paper out of my backpack and begin drawing circles. Squiggly lines, round shapes.

"Everything is going to be fine," I say, more to myself than to them.

Vicious Sid pats me on the back while Sheila and Corso and Bojack-Runt tell me over and over it's going to be fine, everything is going to be fine.

It's only when lunch ends that I realize I still haven't talked to Alice.

The rest of the afternoon I hurry from class to class, too worried people will remark about the incident. Luckily nobody brings it up.

In art, my favorite class, I finally start to settle down a little bit and relax. We draw apples and shade them with our pencils. I draw eyes on mine. I draw a baby apple and a mom apple.

In language arts, Ms. Blakely talks about Greek mythology and folktales. "The Chupacabra eats goats and pigs and cattle," she says. She shows us illustrations on the projector screen.

"Chupacabras are real," a boy named Adler says. "My grandpa says it's a coyote with mange or some kind of beast."

I'm still drowsy from lunch, but the spookiness of the drawings on the screen holds my interest.

"The trickster Chupacabra," Ms. Blakely says. "It's like a vampire in the night."

She shows images of Greek gods, creatures, Odysseus fighting the Cyclops.

"In a past life I was an animal," a kid named George says. He is wearing a yellow shirt with blue stripes. He gets up and walks over to the window. We watch him to see what he'll do, but he just sits by the window and looks out.

"You were a donkey," Adler tells him. "Or a goat. Or a mule. Maybe you were a raccoon."

"I think everyone is an animal," George says. "We're all animals, right, Ms. Blakely?"

"Actually, well . . ." Ms. Blakely says.

"We have a pug named Marlon Brando who snores," a boy named Kayden interrupts.

"My mom disappeared," I tell them. "I think if she became anything, it was a bird."

Everyone looks at me. Most of the kids in class know about my mom, but it's still awkward whenever I bring it up. Yet for some reason I like to remind them.

"It was so long ago," I say. "I was a baby, so I don't even remember her."

Ms. Blakely pauses the projector and starts to say something, but the bell rings and everyone rushes out. I take my books and hurry out of the classroom, too.

My next class is drama. We're reading Shakespeare's *A Midsummer Night's Dream* aloud, but I have trouble understanding what's happening.

"The language can be hard," Ms. Sedona tells us, "so we have to really look closely to see all the puns Shakespeare was using."

She dims the lights, and we watch the movie, which makes it more enjoyable—except I still can't figure out what's happening. Ms. Sedona stops the video every five minutes or so to explain to us what's going on. There are magic potions and people falling in love and chasing each other around, and soon it becomes enjoyable.

In history, Mr. Lynch talks about the Indian Removal Act that led to the Trail of Tears. He passes out maps for us to draw the trails out of Georgia, westward to Oklahoma. The questions at the bottom are easy: *Define "Colonialism." Define "Indian Removal Act." Name the Five Civilized Tribes. Why did Andrew Jackson remove Native Americans from their land?*

I write: *Andrew Jackson and white settlers stole the land. They were responsible for killing thousands of Cherokees.*

I write: *Dragging Canoe warned us that the soldiers were coming.*

I write: *I have dreams of people being forced from their houses and led to stockades. In these dreams I see a line of wagons. I see dust and smoke rising to a hazy sky.*

Mr. Lynch has crazy cool gray hair. I've seen him between classes outside, smoking cigarettes. He wears black dress shirts buttoned to the neck. Today in class, he powers up his computer and projects images of the various trails on the board. The class works quietly on their maps.

"I can tell you this was an absolute tragedy," Mr. Lynch says. "I know I'm not a Native American, but it was bad."

He stares into the light of his computer monitor as he continues talking about the horrific event. I see his jowls sagging, his intense gaze as he talks about the tribes.

"The Cherokees, the Choctaws," he says. "The suffering. Can you imagine? I can't. Let's read from Andrew Jackson's second annual address to Congress in 1830, shall we? Who wants to read aloud? How about you, Sid?"

I look over at Vicious Sid, who sits straight up in his chair, looking terrified. He shakes his head.

"Oh, come on," Mr. Lynch urges him. "Buck up and be a man."

Vicious Sid still shakes his head, looking down at his desk.

Mr. Lynch puts his hands on his hips. I think it's his gesture for being annoyed. I see coaches put their hands on their hips all the time whenever they talk to their players. Is it a way of intimidating them? Why do so many guy teachers and coaches have to put their hands on their hips whenever they talk?

"I'll read," Bojack-Runt speaks up, looking around. "If that's okay with everyone? As long as nobody objects?"

Nobody cares, so Mr. Lynch motions for him to proceed.

"'The consequences of a speedy removal will be important to the United States, to individual states, and to the Indians themselves . . .'"

I stare out the window and zone out. Then I hear Alice speak up.

"Andrew Jackson looks just like a weasel," she says.

Everyone laughs.

Mr. Lynch goes over to Alice's desk and puts his hands on his hips, but he doesn't say anything.

Bojack-Runt continues, "'. . . separate the Indians from immediate contact with settlements of whites.'" He looks up at Mr. Lynch. "He's talking about us."

"Correct," Mr. Lynch says, glancing around the room. "The Native Americans."

Bojack-Runt looks over at me and we try not to laugh at Mr. Lynch.

Mr. Lynch crosses his arms and rocks on his heels. "Some of the Native Americans remained and hid in the mountains. Did you know that?"

"The Nunnehi helped the Cherokees," Alice says. "They were the spirits who presented themselves in human form. My grandpa tells stories about them. One story was about a boy who was setting a fish trap on the river one day when a man approached him and invited him to his home to eat dinner. The man said he lived by a cornfield and an orchard. The boy was nervous but followed the man to his home anyway—"

"This sounds dangerous," Mr. Lynch interrupts. "Was the boy kidnapped? Did he never return home? Disappear?"

"No," Alice tells him. "He was greeted by the man's kids and family, and he ate with them. They were nice to him. Later, as he walked home past the orchard and cornfield, he turned around but didn't see the orchard or cornfield. There were only trees. So he knew they were Nunnehi. But when he returned home, his parents and family were really afraid because he was gone for so long."

I find Alice's story fascinating and hopeful; it's one that I haven't heard before.

"Well, really," Mr. Lynch says, looking skeptical. "You know, I find those old stories fascinating, but they're not real. They're fiction. Folklore. I mean, seriously, Alice, it's not like you were there or anything."

"Oh sure," Alice says, twisting her hair. "Whatever you say."

"It was such a horrific event," Mr. Lynch says, rehearsed, staring into his monitor.

His face is serious, like he's in the middle of a world championship chess match. Or like he's shooting a free throw in game seven of the NBA Finals and everything rests on his last shot.

"The suffering was intense," he says.

It's awkward listening to Mr. Lynch try to teach Native history, especially about our ancestors. I suppose it's good that he's at least trying, though. Better to at least try than to not teach it at all.

"Yep," Mr. Lynch says. "It was horrible."

"Tell us all about it," Alice says again, twisting her hair.

When the bell rings and school is out, Alice meets me by my locker and asks whether I want to walk with her down the street to Baskin-Robbins.

"I don't have any money," I tell her.

"It doesn't matter. I have some."

I'm too embarrassed to say I can't pay her back, so I hesitate.

"It's no big deal," she insists. "Let's just go."

"I need to tell my dad this time. He picks me up since Moon is at a drama club meeting."

My dad is rarely late, but I don't see him anywhere in the parking lot. Alice sits on the steps with me while we wait. For the first time, I notice Alice is wearing blue jeans with small rips in the knees. I know this is fashionable because Moon has a pair of jeans like this. Alice catches me staring and asks, "Do you like these jeans?"

I don't say anything. The bus pulls out of the lot and rumbles away, exhaust chugging behind it.

"They're comfortable," she goes on. "I walk a lot in them. I'm glad I live close enough to walk to school. I would hate riding the bus."

"I used to ride it," I say, but I regret telling her this because right away I know what she's going to ask.

"Why don't you anymore?"

I don't want to tell her that I quit riding the bus because some of the eighth-grade boys once stole my backpack and tossed it around. I'd told them there were poisonous baby snakes inside it, and when they opened it and found my Rubik's Cube, they threatened to throw it out the window. The bus driver wore earphones and never paid any attention.

"Well," I say, "my dad can take off work to come get me now."

"I was thinking about what you said yesterday," she says. "About the caves. What if it's the wrong cave?"

"What do you mean?"

"I mean what if it's not the cave you're looking for? It may not be the cave that leads you to find anything concerning your mom."

I think about this. It occurs to me she may be right.

"Well, we'll just have to keep looking," I say.

"You still want to see a secret cave?"

"One hundred percent yes. Can we go tonight? It's Friday, so no school tomorrow."

"I'm worried the cave won't help you," she says. "I don't want you to be disappointed."

"I guess we can just try."

"Ziggy, I know what it's like to have people laugh at you."

I turn away, embarrassed. She saw me trip in the cafeteria at lunch, but I don't bring it up.

"Hey," she says, "I have a stupid hearing aid. People call me Weird Alice, whatever. It's fine. I don't really care anymore."

I turn to her, but I can't look her in the eyes. It's the way I am. It doesn't mean I don't like talking to people. Kids used to laugh at me for always looking at my feet or at my hands when I talked to people. It isn't too bad with my friends, but it feels difficult to look at Alice in the eyes for some reason.

"I don't care either," I lie.

We fall quiet. The silence is awkward, at least for me, but it's quickly broken by my dad blaring the horn of his pickup.

"There he is," I say, standing and putting my backpack on.

"Ask him if you can come with me," she says.

But Dad is already sticking his head out the window and yelling for me to hurry up. I run over to the pickup on his side and ask him if I can walk to Baskin-Robbins.

"What?" he says. "Not today. Your grandma needs your help."

"Help with what?"

"Just get in," he says. "We have to hurry."

"One sec," I say to Dad. Then I run back over to Alice and tell her, "I'm sorry I can't go with you. My dad says I have to go help my grandma. But what about the cave?"

"See you tonight," Alice says, then runs away.

I hurry back to the pickup and get in. Dad tells me to put on my seat belt and then steps on the gas pedal, jolting me in my seat, peeling out so that the tires squeal.

"What's the deal?" I say. "What's wrong with Grandma?"

My dad doesn't answer, which is strange. We drive down Cherry Street, past the football field and baseball diamond until we reach a curve and my dad takes it fast. I have to hold on to the door handle.

"Is she okay?" I ask.

I'm starting to worry that something terrible has happened to my grandma. I have a terrible feeling in my stomach, like maybe she has disappeared or even died, and I feel my heart begin to race.

My dad straightens the steering wheel and hits the gas, and as I look out the window it feels like the trees are flying by at a higher speed than normal even though I know they're not. My heart is pounding and there's a burning in my stomach. I see poisonberries everywhere outside. I hear the gravel underneath the tires as he slows to a stop sign near our house. Then he presses the gas again, and I close my eyes as he speeds up and takes a quick turn on our street. I'm afraid my grandma is dead, gone forever like my mom, and it feels terrifying.

"I don't want Grandma to die!" I say. "Please, Dad!"

Dad slows the truck and turns in to our drive. He pulls up and kills the engine and looks at me.

"What are you talking about?" he asks. I realize I've bitten the inside of my mouth from being so scared, and now I'm too afraid to even move.

Dad opens his door and gets out. He comes over to my side and opens the door and looks at me. "Well?" he says. "Are you coming? What's wrong?"

"What's wrong with Grandma?"

"Ziggy," he says, helping me out of the truck and taking my backpack for me. "Your grandma is fine. Let's go inside."

I take my backpack and hurry inside the house, where I hear loud big-band music playing. It's the type of big-band music that's popular with old people. Then I can't believe what I see: My grandma is dancing. Alone.

I stand there, watching her, and she turns to see me. "Come dance with me," she says, holding her arms out.

"Oh no, please, no."

"Come on," she says.

She does the twist, the shimmy, then dances over to me and takes my hands.

"I feel great!" she says.

That makes one of us. I'm still recovering from my panic in the car.

All evening I keep thinking my grandma must be confused. I don't understand why she would be so happy to dance by herself. Or maybe I'm overreacting the way Kari says I do sometimes. I remember telling her once that a video on the Internet showed part of a rocket ship in outer space heading directly for Earth, and I was convinced it would land right on our house.

"Has anything like that ever happened before?" Kari asked me.

"Not that I know of."

"So it's probably not going to happen, right?"

I had to stop reading articles online for science class because every time I found an article, it horrified me so badly I couldn't fall asleep. My dad would have to come lie down with me and try to echo what Kari had told me, but it didn't help me feel better. I'm not sure what made me feel better except time passing.

"It's possible that anything dangerous can happen at any minute," I told my dad.

"I guess anything is possible," he said. "But it isn't probable."

I had to think about that for a long time, but soon, very slowly, things started to make sense whenever I considered probability over possibility.

Then again, there were some things my imagination ran away with, for whatever reason, and left me terrified.

(((7)))

The Nunnehi

Grandma makes some sort of weird casserole for dinner that tastes like a rubber tire, so I don't eat very much and end up sneaking a package of peanuts from the pantry when nobody's looking. After supper, she tells Moon and me stories about my mom when she was a little girl. One thing I like about Grandma is that she loves telling us stories about Mom.

"Your mom used to chase a rabbit around in our backyard when she was little," Grandma tells us. "She could never catch that rabbit. Even our dog, Frog, couldn't catch it."

"Wait a minute," Moon says. "You had a dog named Frog?"

Grandma sits in a cloud of smoke, puffing on her pipe. "And a frog named Dog. Well, the frog wasn't really our pet. It lived in the backyard, too. We had a whole wonderland of varmints out there. A rabbit, a frog, a mouse, a feral cat. A caterpillar that smoked a hookah."

Dad has fallen asleep in the recliner, snoring every now and then. The smoke around Grandma rises as she leans forward with a serious expression on her face.

"Ziggy," she says, "you seem worried about something."

I glance at Moon, who is also staring at me. I'm still giving her the silent treatment, which doesn't seem to bother her. This only infuriates me more.

"It's nothing," I say.

"He's worried," Moon says. "He wants to go explore the desert."

Our dad coughs in his sleep, then continues snoring.

"For what?"

"I don't know," I answer before Moon can. "Mom liked to explore the desert and look for secret caves, so I want to do it, too."

Grandma looks at me with concern. She usually says something random or changes the subject whenever we want to talk about our mom's disappearance.

"You know the story of the Nunnehi who live in caves?" she asks.

"You always tell us about them," we say, but she goes on like it's the first time.

"I love good tobacco and good stories," she says, closing her eyes. A braid of smoke chugs from her pipe and turns into the form of a snake as it rises to the ceiling. "The Nunnehi are spirits who helped Cherokees hide in caves before the removal. Storytellers. Good ones, too. They protect and they help us, still around wherever Cherokee families are. They can travel any-where in the world, kids. They can take the form of people and look human, so you never know when you might see one."

"Are you saying they're here in New Mexico?" I ask.

She removes the pipe from her mouth. "It's very likely they are. Do you keep your eyes open for them? I imagine you've seen many of them without even knowing it. But they're most active in the middle of the night, and I go to bed early. You have to catch them when they're playing music and dancing. That's when they're happiest."

"Can they disguise themselves as animals?" I ask.

"Maybe so. What animal would you like to be?"

"A shark," I say.

"A shark," Grandma says. "Why a shark?"

I'm not sure why. Maybe because they're vicious and power-ful, always moving. They're not timid or afraid—not anything like me.

I tell Grandma, "They get to swim all the time."

Our dad wakes up from his chair and runs a hand over his face. "Sounds good," he says, pretending he hasn't fallen asleep. "I better go take a shower."

"You were snoring," Moon tells him.

"Me? Nah. Just rested my eyes for a minute."

"You snored for half an hour."

"Me? Nah."

"We sat here and heard you the whole time," she says.

"Me?" He gets up slowly and we hear his bones creak. He

walks stiffly to his bedroom. Grandma stands from the cloud of smoke around her rocking chair and tells us goodnight.

"Wait a minute," I say. I hurry into my bedroom and find my mini basketball. I do a quick turnaround jump shot, then a one-handed dunk, then a two-handed dunk. When I'm done, Grandma is standing in the doorway.

"I have to do my basketball shots before bed," I tell her. "It's a nightly ritual. Last night it was too late by the time I remembered, so I had to pretend to do them in the living room."

"If you ever find the Nunnehi, ask them to play," she says. "They love playing games."

"What kind of games?"

"All kinds. But mostly hide-and-seek. I saw a Nunnehi when I was little. It was a little girl who played hide-and-seek with me all afternoon one day, not long after my little brother passed of pneumonia."

"How did you know she was a Nunnehi?" I ask.

"She told me to close my eyes and count to three and when I opened them she would disappear. But I cheated and opened them after one second, and when I opened my eyes she was already gone, just like that, in the blink of an eye."

"Did you ever see her again?"

"Who knows?" she says. "But I've always sensed she's close by."

I think about this, and I can tell it pleases Grandma. Her stories always make me think.

I tell her goodnight, toss the basketball on the floor, and

return to the living room. Moon is sitting in the recliner, texting on her phone.

"You're mad at me," she says, still looking at her phone. "It's so obvious."

"You gave up on me," I tell her. "You don't even want to try to explore the desert."

She takes a deep breath. "Where did you put that sketchbook Grandma gave you?" she asks.

"In my room. Why?"

"She didn't give me anything," Moon says.

"She didn't bring you anything?"

Moon shakes her head. "It's not a big deal or anything."

Moon keeps texting on her phone, and I sit on the couch and play my Nintendo Switch. While I'm playing, I begin to feel sad for Moon. Why would Grandma give me something of Mom's and not Moon?

"Maybe Grandma will give you something else that was Mom's," I tell her.

She shrugs, then gets up and disappears into her room.

I change into my pajamas, then turn off the light and put my headphones on. Listening to music helps me fall asleep, but I suddenly feel drowsy enough that I know it won't take me long to drift off. I listen first to French pop, then jazz.

Just as the sound of the slow saxophone and trumpet lulls me to sleep, I hear a knocking at the window.

Someone is outside on the porch.

(((8)))

An Old Buzzard

There's a figure at the window. I sit up in bed and look closer to see a person looking in the window, which is terrifying, but then I can tell it's a girl. I turn on the lamp and step over to the window. To my surprise, I see it's Alice.

"Ziggy!" she says, waving me to her. "Hey, Ziggy, come out here."

I hold up a finger to signal for her to wait so I can put on my shoes and my hoodie. Quietly, I unlock the front door and step outside.

Alice emerges out of the darkness, dressed in a white nightgown and black boots, looking like a ghost in the night. I can't believe she's here this late at night.

"Alice," I say quietly. "What are you doing here? It's late. And you're in your nightgown."

She takes a step toward me, and I can see her face, paler in the porch light. "I had to sneak out of my window," she says. "I brought my friend Rango. He's a coyote, but don't worry, he won't hurt you."

She points to the yard, where I see a small, thin coyote cowering.

"My name is Chupacabra," the coyote says from the darkness. "Not Rango."

This animal speaks English? And in such a raspy voice. Am I awake? Dreaming? Does it matter? I'm worried the coyote is dangerous, so I take a step back toward the door.

"His name isn't Chupacabra," she says. "Don't let him fool you—he's harmless. His name is Rango."

She hurries to the yard, kneels, and scratches him on the head. "Oh, Rango, stop with your tricks. You don't fool anyone."

"I'm a Chupacabra going back to the desert," Rango says. "You'll find me if you whistle. Or maybe I'll find you."

"I can't whistle," I say. "Alice, what is he talking about?"

"You have to use both pinkies," Alice tells me, "just like this." She puts both pinkies in her mouth and whistles so loudly we hear dogs bark and howl in the distance.

"Quiet!" I tell her. "You want to wake everyone? What time is it?"

She looks at her watch. "Not even eleven."

I sit down on the steps in front of her. "All right," I say. "So what's up? What are you doing here so late?"

"Let's go find a secret cave," she says. "Like we talked about earlier today."

"Tonight? Right now?"

She twirls in the night. "Why not? It'll be fun, Ziggy."

"But—I don't know."

She steps closer and looks serious. "You told me you're stuck in the past, worried about your mom. Why not take a journey and see what we can find?"

"Oh wow," I say. My heart races. I'm not sure whether I should go with her, which could lead to trouble. What if somebody found us walking around? What if the police caught us and arrested us for breaking a curfew? My dad would kill me.

"Trust Alice," Rango says, licking his paw. He shakes himself like a wet dog, then slinks away into the night.

"Bye, Rango," Alice tells him. "Maybe we'll see you later."

I take a breath. "Wait, how long will we be gone? I can't stay out all night."

"Be cool," she says, stepping over and sitting on the steps beside me. "It'll be fine if you trust me. I'll protect you, don't worry."

All I can think about is walking in that darkness by the light of our phones. The crazy people and creatures of the night will be out sniffing for fresh human blood. Above us, moonlight casts a long and fractured shadow from the garage onto the front lawn.

"Maybe we should wait until daylight," I suggest.

"Why? Are you scared?"

"A little. Do the crazies come out at night?"

"Don't be silly," she says, bunching the fabric of her nightgown in her hands as if she's restless and on edge. "It's

Poisonberry, the most boring place on earth. When was the last time anything dangerous ever happened here?"

I pull on my bottom lip and try to think about what could happen. It would be an adventure, after all. Maybe we really could find a clue about where my mom disappeared. And Alice seems sincere, even if she's different.

I agree, which makes her squeal in delight.

"Do I need anything?" I ask. "I only have my phone."

"I think that's all you need," she says, and we stand from the steps.

As we head down the street, I see a bluer, darker world all around, a beckoning world of adobe houses and twisting paths, the street glimmering with yellow spots from the streetlights. The moon is full and pale, the air dense with moonlight. I walk looking up at the moon with a dizzy exhilaration.

"You're walking too slow," Alice tells me. "You want to take all night?"

The streetlights along Cheshire Street keep us from having to use our phones for any light. Alice and I walk along the sidewalk, heading north toward Main Street. Poisonberry vines twist around trees like snakes in the night, spilling onto the sidewalk. It doesn't bother Alice to step on them even when I warn her.

"I'm immune to them," she says. "I forgot to tell you—they don't bother me."

"Me too," I say. "I used to eat them when I was little. So did Moon."

"I used to smear them on my mouth for lipstick," she says.

"So did we. We got in trouble for eating them."

"I tried to poison a bad man once," she says, waving her hands in the night as if we're walking in a parade. "I put the berries in his tea when he visited my mother."

"Did it make him sick?"

"It made him go away," she says. "He was already evil. He was trying to hurt someone I was protecting. The berries made him sick, but he didn't die."

I want to ask her who the bad man is, and why he wanted to hurt someone, but it doesn't feel appropriate.

Up ahead we notice something move in the trees beside a two-story brick house set back from the street. I stop walking and Alice turns to me.

"Something moved in the trees," I tell her, pointing ahead.

She takes a step forward and looks. We wait for it to move again, but the tree is still.

"It's nothing bad," she says. "What do you think you saw?"

"It's too dark, but something moved."

"A figure? Like a person?"

"In the trees," I say. "Like something hiding in the trees."

"Probably just birds," she says. "Come on."

We cross the street and head east, though I keep looking back at the trees. Maybe my mind is playing tricks, like when you think you see a ghost in your room at night, but it's really headlights flashing across the wall from a car driving by. That used to happen a lot when I was little. Every night, headlights flashed across my wall.

It's not so bad anymore. I still dress up for Halloween and go trick-or-treating. I just don't like haunted houses or things jumping out at me or being startled in any way.

"There's nothing to worry about," Alice keeps telling me.

I feel restless and awake. We walk quickly, which feels invigorating to me. There's something about walking at night that I don't feel whenever I walk in the daylight—maybe the sun zaps all my energy or something.

We walk by quiet houses with dark windows and cars parked in driveways, past lawns lit from bright porch lights. We pass elm trees and maple trees with low-hanging branches and small piles of leaves scattered around them. I can't believe I'm not in the least bit tired. In fact, it seems as though the more we walk, the more energy I have. The night is especially glowing and translucent, heavy with the smell of sugar maples and woodsmoke.

"Tonight the world is blue," Alice says. "Look around. Isn't it beautiful?"

She's right: Everything in the moonlight looks blue. The sky, all the houses, even the street.

"Look at the silver trees," I say, pointing to the maple trees across the street. Then I see something move there. This time Alice sees it, too.

"Oh wow," she says. "What is that? It's a person in the tree? Wait—maybe it's the wind moving the branches?"

My heart races. We stand there watching for something to

move, to see someone, something—but nothing else happens.

"Maybe it's the wind," I say, still watching. "The moon is bright."

"Let's keep walking," Alice says.

I find myself looking up into the sky and staggering again, but this time Alice doesn't notice and a moment later I'm out in the middle of the road.

"Ziggy," she says. "Hey, look. We're on Corso's street."

Sure enough, I see Corso's house at the end of the block under the glowing streetlight. How strange we arrive there so quickly. Alice looks determined, serious as she walks, motioning for me to follow.

"Corso's probably in bed," I say.

But as we get closer to his house, I'm surprised to see him standing on the front porch with his guitar. I call out his name—"Hey, Corso!" He sees us and waves.

We hurry to him, and he comes into the yard to meet us.

"What are you doing here?" he asks. "It's late."

"Alice is taking me to the place where I might find my mom, or some hint about where she went," I tell him.

"Oh," he says. He looks at Alice.

"A secret cave," I say.

"Oh," Corso says again. "That's cool, Ziggy."

"Why don't you come with us?" I ask.

Alice agrees. "Yeah, we need someone else anyway in case someone chases us or something, right? Safety in numbers."

Corso thinks a minute, then goes over and sits on the

porch steps. We follow and sit beside him. I can tell something's wrong. Why else would he be outside by himself at this hour?

"I have to do that dumb report in history class for Mr. Lynch," he says. "My parents told me I had to work on it tonight because we're supposed to be doing stuff all weekend. I tried, I swear. After they fell asleep I needed a break, so I snuck into the kitchen and grabbed a box of Pop-Tarts and ate them out here."

"The report for Lynch's history class?" Alice says. "No problem. You could write it on Monday morning before school. He likes short and weird reports. I'll probably write mine Sunday night."

"But you know it has to be something unique we research about the Trail of Tears," he says. "Easy for you guys since you already know about that stuff, being Native and all. I'm a white dude."

"You can talk to the Nunnehi with us," I tell him. "They'll help you come up with something. Right, Alice?"

Alice looks at me, her face heavy with uncertainty.

"Who knows?" she says. "The Nunnehi may not be there. But I'll at least show you the secret cave so that you'll know where to find them."

"What about my project?" Corso asks her.

"You have to come with us if you want help," Alice tells Corso.

Corso turns around and looks to the front door. All the windows in the house are dark and the house sits silent.

"I guess so," he says. "My parents are in bed, so they shouldn't know anything. Let's go before I change my mind."

It makes Alice and me happy, and we all spring from the porch and run into the night like ghosts.

We aren't far from Corso's when we hear music coming from somewhere in the distance. Past his street, in an empty field that leads out of town, there's a light flickering as if someone is trying to signal us.

"What's that light up ahead?" I ask. "See it in the field? I wonder if that's where the music is coming from?"

"It sounds like old-people music," Alice says. "Like the music my grandparents listen to."

"Old-people music?" I say.

"Everybody, wait a minute," Corso says. "It's a fiddle."

We stop walking and listen. We hear someone singing, but we can't hear it well enough to make out the words. Then I see movement, a figure up ahead by the light in the field.

"I see something out there," I tell them. "Maybe we should go back."

Corso seems entranced by the music. His eyes are wide and intense, staring straight ahead as he walks toward the field. I look at Alice, who smiles.

"Corso," I say, keeping up with him, "what's the deal? Are you okay?"

"The music," he says, hypnotized. "The fiddle music."

"What about it, Corso? Alice, what's going on?"

"Don't worry," Alice says. "I'll protect you."

"Protect me from what?"

Alice just laughs in response as we follow Corso.

The figure I saw before is now heading our way. Under a streetlight at the end of the street we all stop walking, and the figure emerges, flying out of the darkness. It's a tall, gangly old buzzard playing a fiddle. He stops playing, puts the fiddle under his wing, and lands right in front of us. He looks at us with bloodshot eyes, and suddenly I want to turn and run away. My heart is racing. It's the biggest buzzard I've ever seen. He stands tall with a long, crooked beak and droopy eyes. His head is big and bald.

"Umm," Alice says.

The old buzzard opens his mouth and speaks: "Y'all headed out yonder to find the Storyteller?"

I'm too afraid to talk. Corso snaps out of his trance and asks, "What was the tune you were playing on that fiddle?"

The buzzard speaks slowly and in a deep voice: "It's called 'Loretta.' Why?"

"Wait a second," Alice says. "Who's the Storyteller? And why do you want to know where we're going, you nosy bird?"

Corso and I both look hard at Alice. Did she just call this giant buzzard nosy? Is she not as afraid as I am?

"The Storyteller supposedly lives out yonder by the caves," the old buzzard says, swallowing. His neck is thin and bulging. "The Storyteller's got some stories to tell folks around here. Takes them up in hot-air-balloon rides."

"We're not interested," Alice tells him. "We're on our way to see something else. So if you'll excuse us, we'll continue our walk."

"I was kicked out of my house by the government," the buzzard says. "They told me to leave. They told all of us buzzards to leave, as a matter of fact."

"Why?" Corso asks.

He shakes his head, disappointed. "The government decided other folks need to live there. The land was theirs, that's what they said. But we were there first. It was our land."

"Couldn't you do anything about it?" Corso asks.

"We tried, but they brought in people and forced us out. See, most of the other buzzards are smaller than me, and the humans—no offense—are big and bullyish. So there was nothing we could do. All I do is drift and sing now. And try to eat roadkill out here. There's no home. We all just live wherever we can. That's the way of the buzzard these days."

Corso, Alice, and I all look at each other, unsure what to say. It's a sad story and the buzzard looks weary and distraught. Dad always said buzzards are important creatures to us, to Cherokees, because they helped create the valleys and mountains of the earth. We should never hurt them or put them in danger.

"Would you play 'Loretta' again?" Corso asks. "Do you mind? Before we go on, I'd like to hear it."

The buzzard agrees despite looking so sleepy-eyed and exhausted. He tucks his fiddle under his beak and begins playing it, then sings in a slow, tuneless voice:

You ever seen a prettier gal than Lor-etta?
Smart as a whip, the anchor of my ship, Lor-etta.
I'm losing sleep, can't think about nothing
but Lor-etta.
Can you hear me crying out for you?
Howling like a gunshot dog?
I know you're gone forever,
But I see that twinkling star in the big sky.
I'll always have memories of you,
Aahooooo-wheeee, aahooooo-wheeee,
My sweet Lor-etta.

"It's haunting," Corso says, glancing at me.

"Name's Gus," the old buzzard replies.

"Wait—your name is Gus?" Alice asks.

Gus the fiddle-playing buzzard bows in gratitude, then looks at me, as if waiting for me to say something, too, but I'm not sure what to say. I don't know whether it's beautiful or sad. It sounds like a song my dad would sing for my mom. I don't know what to think, really. All I can say is: "Weeiirrd?"

Gus sets his fiddle on the ground and steps over to me, which is frightening, so I take a step back. He's taller than me—taller than all three of us, and he leans forward so that his big, crooked beak is directly in front of me. My heart is still racing.

"*Weird* is the best compliment you can give someone," he says in a low voice.

I don't understand.

He steps back and speaks to all of us. "My whole life, people have called me weird. I'm lankier than most buzzards."

I look at Alice and Corso and see they're both entranced by the old buzzard, staring at him in wonder.

"Weirdos are good," he goes on. "When people call me weird, I'm proud. It's good to be different. I'm myself, that's who I am. I sing because I love to sing. I play fiddle because I love it. I don't care what people think anymore. That song, 'Loretta,' I wrote it for my wife, who passed away many years ago."

This poor buzzard lost his wife, just like my dad lost his.

"Did you have kids?" I ask.

Gus shakes his head. "Never did, but I have memories of the time Loretta and I spent together. Where did y'all say you was headed?"

"Well," Alice says, "we're actually going to a secret cave."

"What fer?"

"Ummm," Alice says, and then hesitates, looking at me.

"To explore for clues to find my mom," I say.

I explain about how my mom loved to explore the desert at night, so we're doing the same thing.

"You never know if you'll find the Nunnehi," he says. "They're tricksters. They can disguise themselves as humans or animals—you never know. Sometimes we have to accept that things don't always work out the way we planned."

"What do you mean?" I ask him.

"Aliheliga," Gus says. "Be grateful fer what you got, son.

Don't get discouraged, and be grateful for memories. It's all we have after people are gone."

I'm not sure I believe him, or why he's telling us this. Nobody whistled or called out for him. He just showed up.

In the streetlight I can see his eyes are bloodshot. He looks at a watch he's wearing on one of his legs. "It's almost midnight," he says.

We thank him for his time. He gives us a slight wave and then turns and flies away, playing the fiddle as he disappears into the dark field.

"Gus, the fiddle-playing buzzard," Corso says. "Oh man, nobody will believe it."

"That was strange," I say. "I don't understand why he told us all that stuff about the Storyteller. Is that someone we should be afraid of?"

Alice shrugs. "I've never seen such a person. All I know is how to get to the cave."

"I'm not sure I buy it. He seemed suspicious."

"He means be yourself, Ziggy," Alice says. "Hold on to memories of people you've lost. Like your mom, right? It makes sense."

But I was too little to have any memories of my mom. Still, I want to see her now more than ever, so I'm ready to continue our trek to the cave, or to find any other clues we can.

"We don't have to cross the field, do we?" Corso says. "I've heard coyotes howling out there. My dad says he once saw a bobcat roaming around. I never go there at night."

"Yeah, but we have to go in the opposite direction," Alice tells him. "Gus went right; we need to go left and follow a trail that leads to Old Hickory Road, about half a mile."

Corso thinks a minute. "Old Hickory Road? Can't we get there a different way?"

"Not unless you want to walk all the way back past the school and make a U-turn, which would be tiring and lose us time."

"But the field?" Corso is terrified. "What about coyotes? What about bobcats?"

While they argue about all this, I see something move in a large maple tree across the street. "Look!" I cry, interrupting them. They stop talking to look in the direction I'm pointing.

We see rustling, someone in the tree, watching us. I can see the shape of a figure, even in the darkness. As I watch, it falls out of the tree.

"Oh no!" Alice says. "Someone fell—let's go help!"

We hurry across the street to where the person is lying on her stomach on the grass beside the base of the tree. Her hair spills over the grass.

We can't believe what we see.

It's Moon.

(((9)))

The Strange Armadillo

Everyone give her room to breathe," Corso says. He's trying to get Moon to sit up while Alice looks at me for help.

I take Moon's hand and hold it in mine. "Moon," I say, but her eyes are closed and her lips are pursed, like she's having a bad dream she can't wake from. Once we get her to sit up, though, her eyes slowly open and she blinks.

"Moon," I say again. "Hey, are you okay?"

"I'm fine." She squints and touches her cheek. "I lost my balance, I guess. How did you know it was me in the tree?"

"We didn't. What are you doing here? Why were you up there?"

"I was watching you guys. I followed you from home, Ziggy."

We help her to her feet and brush off the leaves from her shirt and arms. Moon staggers a moment, a little uneasy.

"You sure you're okay?" Corso asks.

Moon takes a deep breath and hooks a strand of hair behind her ear. "It wasn't the fall that made me dizzy," she tells us. "It must've been the adrenaline."

"Huh?"

"It's like, the moment I stepped outside to follow you guys, I had all this amazing energy. So I ran across the street and climbed a tree, then another, and soon I totally forgot I was even following you guys. Does that sound weird?"

"Yes," Corso and I say at the same time.

Out of nowhere, Moon steps closer and embraces me. She hugs me for a long time, without saying anything, and I'm not sure how to even respond, so I just hug her back.

Then she pulls away and looks at me. "I'm sorry for what I said yesterday about giving up hope to find Mom."

"It's fine," I say.

"No, it isn't. I want to go with you now. Sound good?"

A gust of wind blows and nearly knocks me over. We hear bells ring from a church in the distance, and Corso looks at his watch. "Oh man, it's midnight and I'm not even one bit tired."

"Nobody's tired, and it's so windy," Alice says, her hair in her face from the wind. "You guys still want to go to the cave?"

"Yes!" we all say, so Alice leads the way to the dirt trail toward Old Hickory Road. We walk in single file, poisonberries stretched out all around us. I tell everyone to be careful and stay on the trail. "Corso, don't step in any berries or it will ruin everything," I tell him.

"I'm fine!" he calls back.

The wind is howling worse, it seems. I'm worried about all the poisonberry shrubs around blowing in the wind and entering our lungs, but I don't say anything to anyone about it because they'll just tell me I'm acting ridiculous. The worst thing that could happen is Corso breathing in poisonberry seeds and dying out here right in front of us.

"Everyone cover your mouth!" I shout.

Alice nudges me. "I'll protect you," she says.

"Why do you keep saying that?" I ask her.

Alice smiles and continues walking.

Old Hickory Road runs parallel to the field and curves around an abandoned white church and vacant gas station lot, leading out of town. Once we make it to the road, it feels as though we've already entered a new dimension because the road is shiny and silver under the moonlight.

"Look at the road," Corso says. "It looks like we're walking on glass."

"Or water," I add.

Alice says the moon does strange things in the night that can create mirages or hallucinations, so we should be careful about what we see. "There's something that happens out here in the wind," she warns. "The wind howls and swirls. Things fly around in a circular motion."

"Like what?" I ask.

"Tornadoes, trash, leaves—even houses. Anything, really."

As we continue walking, sure enough, I see a spinning gust

of wind above us. "Look at the sky," I call out to everyone. "What is it?"

"It looks like a small tornado," Moon says. "It's lowering, too."

The whirlwind reaches toward the ground in the distance. I know how destructive tornadoes can be. Tornadoes have no feelings of guilt or remorse about their devastation. They'll sweep through and flatten buildings and houses and then lift back into the sky.

We stop walking and look in the distance, the moonlight making everything visible. The tornado is touching the ground, spraying dust all around.

"We need to find shelter!" Moon calls out to everyone. "In there—let's hurry." She points to the abandoned gas station off the road, and we follow her.

We all hurry from the road and run to the building. Corso tries the front doors, but they're locked. We look in the window and don't see much inside. "I'll try around the side," Corso says, then goes around the building. While he's gone, I keep looking inside the window and spot several half-eaten carrots on the floor, along with empty jugs of milk.

"It looks like someone's been in there eating carrots and drinking milk," I say.

We all stare inside the window, but it's hard because the wind is blowing dust around.

"Hopefully not a murderer," Moon says. "We have to go inside."

We hear Corso call out, "Hey, guys, come back!"

We step past old tires and piles of scrap metal to the back of the building, where Corso is standing with the back door open. It's dark inside and he's using his phone as a flashlight to see.

"Be careful," Moon tells him. "There might be rats or something."

"Rats?" Corso gulps, looking back at us.

He flinches and lets the door close. I can see he looks afraid, and I'm a little worried, too, about rats or snakes or something inside an old, abandoned gas station.

"Oh, just move aside," Alice says, stepping past him. She opens the door and we see only darkness, but there's a streetlight that helps keep the lot somewhat lit. Moon finds a rock and wedges the door open, and we all follow Alice inside.

"We only need to stay here until this storm passes," Corso says. We're all flashing our phone lights around, looking for anything more dangerous or deadly than a tornado. Outside, the trees are waving as the wind picks up. We know how to take tornado precaution: Sit on your knees, lean forward, and put your hands on the back of your head. We've done it in school tornado drills for as long as we've been in school.

"I don't hear any sirens," Moon says. "Are we sure it was a tornado?"

"It looked like a small one," I say.

"Are you sure?"

"Not really."

The wind knocks over something outside, and I can see the

branches moving, but there's no rain or thunder, no sirens. "Someone check your phone for the weather," Moon tells us.

"No service," Corso says.

Right then we hear a loud clap of thunder that makes Alice scream. It starts raining and the wind is rattling cans around in the lot outside. We all huddle in the middle of the room and try to get service on our phones, but none of us has any luck. The wind is howling and it's raining harder. The moonlight has disappeared and everything is darker.

I feel my anxiety building, but I'm not sure what to do. I don't have any paper to draw on, so I just try to breathe slowly.

"I love you guys," I tell everyone. It comes out before I realize it, corny as it sounds. And for some reason I'm on the verge of tears. That happens sometimes; I feel like I might start crying. I never know why—it just happens.

"Ziggy, we love you, too," Moon says.

"We all love you, Ziggy," Alice says, and she comes over and puts her arm around me. "We love you, and I'll protect you."

"I'm not scared," I tell them.

We all huddle, listening to the rain patter against the roof and windows. The sound of rain at night always makes me want to go to sleep, and I feel a sudden urge to be back home in my bed under the covers, even if Grandma is sleeping beside me. The fear strikes me and I let out a moan, but then I feel Moon's hand on my back for comfort. She knows how easily I get scared. Why are storms so terrifying? We've never had a bad experience in a storm, never had damage to our house or anything destroyed. Yet my mind creates all these images of catastrophe: a tornado flattening our house, rolling through and sending us to our deaths.

It's anxiety.

Anxiety, panic. This is what Kari would tell me. *Remember probability over possibility. Everything will be fine.*

We are silent as the rain continues, but soon enough it lightens to a sprinkle.

"I think the storm's passed," Alice says.

"I have service," Moon announces, typing on her phone.

"The land is telling us something," Alice says. "Think about it. My dad is always saying the land remembers history."

"What does that even mean?" Corso asks.

"She's right," Moon says to Corso. "It means we need to listen to the land. There's nothing to be afraid of except for rats in here."

As soon as she says it, I see Corso's eyes widen and he screams as loudly and high-pitched as Alice.

His phone shines on something in the corner of the room, and for a second I think it really is a rat. He steps back to the door, and we all shine our phone lights in the corner to see an armadillo cowering in the corner.

"Armadillo!" Corso says. "Gross—look!"

The armadillo shows us his teeth. Armadillos are large rodents with a round, hard shell on their back, and even though they aren't really dangerous, I find them creepy.

"Ugh, gross," Alice says. "He seems afraid. It's okay, everybody. No sudden movements."

We watch it. The armadillo stays in his corner, showing teeth, eyes glowing in the dark. Then he opens his mouth and speaks:

"My name is Andrew Jackson," he hisses, "seventh president of the United States."

Moon turns and looks at the rest of us.

We're all stunned silent by what we've just witnessed.

Finally Moon speaks up: "Um, did that armadillo just talk?"

"That little devil," Alice says.

"Andrew Jackson," I say. "It's Andrew Jackson in the body of an armadillo. He's right here in front of us. How is this real?"

Outside, thunder rumbles quietly in the distance.

"This is the weirdest night of my life," Corso moans. "First, a talking buzzard, and now a talking armadillo. I don't believe it. What's going on tonight?"

We flash our lights at the armadillo. He shivers in the corner of the room, his eyes glowing red.

"To separate," Andrew Jackson hisses. "To separate the Indians from immediate contact with settlements of whites."

"Huh?" Corso says.

Andrew Jackson lowers his snout to the ground, then looks up at us. "To cast off their savage habits."

I remember the speech we read in history class when we were talking about the Trail of Tears and removal of tribes. "It's his speech," I tell everyone. "The State of the Union. Didn't we just learn this in class, Corso?"

Corso doesn't say anything; he looks too afraid.

Alice says, "Yeah, that's right. This was his pathetic reason for genocide."

"I am Andrew Jackson," the armadillo hisses.

I stand behind Corso. We are definitely the cowards of the group. How can an armadillo talk? More important, why would he claim to be Andrew Jackson? I watch him cower there in the corner. I see his red eyes, the pointed snout, the hard shell on his back.

Moon steps forward with her phone, shining it over the armadillo's body so that the armadillo cowers. "You're telling us," she says, "that you're really Andrew Jackson? Seventh president of the United States?"

"I am Andrew Jackson," the armadillo hisses. "A speedy removal will be important to the United States."

"What are you doing here? Can you tell us?"

"Beware the Storyteller."

Alice steps beside Moon and leans in for a closer look. "She asked you a question, Andrew Jackson. What are you doing here?"

"It gives me pleasure," he hisses, "to announce to Congress that the benevolent policy of the Government, steadily pursued for nearly thirty years, in relation to the removal of the Indians beyond the white settlements is approaching to a happy consummation."

"It seems he can't say anything else," Moon says. "He's on an audio loop, saying the same speech over and over."

"He has crazy eyes," Corso says, leaning into me. "What are we supposed to do about this? Call animal control? Let's go."

The armadillo snorts. "What good man would prefer a country covered with forests and ranged by a few thousand savages to our extensive Republic, studded with cities, towns, and prosperous farms, embellished with all the improvements which art can devise or industry execute, occupied by more than twelve million happy people, and filled with the blessings of liberty, civilization, and religion?"

Moon turns to Corso. "Andrew Jackson ordered the removal of Native tribes from their land. They were forced to migrate and leave. They were tricked by the US government."

"But Mr. Lynch didn't even give us the whole speech," I say. "Only parts of it. What was he thinking, leaving so much out? Think about how terrible that is."

The armadillo hisses. "Rightly considered, the policy of the General Government toward the red man is not only liberal, but generous. The General Government kindly offers him a new home. Beware the Storyteller."

"I can't believe this," Corso says. "It's just so totally wrong. And gross! And why is he saying, 'Beware the Storyteller'? The Storyteller, again, like what Gus said earlier."

"You can tell it's Andrew Jackson," Alice says. "Look at his eyes. Also, we should pay attention to truthful storytellers, not beware them. Never listen to anyone who tells us to beware storytellers. Never ever ever."

We stare at Andrew Jackson, the small red eyes, the pointy snout. He makes a snorting sound as he searches for something in the corner.

"It's getting way too creepy in here," Moon says. "I'm going outside."

"To cast off their savage habits," Andrew Jackson says. "A speedy removal . . . Beware the Storyteller."

"Be quiet," Alice tells him, kneeling down and gathering dust and dirt in her hands. Then she opens her palms and blows the dust toward the armadillo. He sneezes.

"A speedy removal," Andrew Jackson hisses.

We follow Moon outside and try to figure out what to do. We hear things rattle and knock from Andrew Jackson rummaging around inside, but he doesn't come out.

"Maybe he's trying to escape from us," I say. "What do we do with him? Capture him and turn him in to animal control? If he doesn't talk, everyone will think we're crazy."

"We could set the building on fire and burn him to death," Alice says, twisting her long hair. "Or we could play tricks on him to confuse him, which would be funny. Anyone want to play tricks?"

"Just toss some poisonberries in there so he'll eat them," I tell her, but then the thought of anything suffering and dying a slow death really makes me feel sick to my stomach, even if it's Andrew Jackson in the body of an armadillo.

"No, no," Alice says. "He's an armadillo. Let him live as an armadillo among all the other rodents and creepy-crawling things out here."

Moon, Corso, and I think about this. Corso and I agree to let Andrew Jackson live among the rodents and garbage out here, but Moon isn't convinced. I can tell she's angry and annoyed.

"Let's go," Alice says, and she and Corso lead the way.

"Not yet," Moon says.

We stop and turn to her.

"This is Andrew Jackson," she says. "Think about that for a minute. Think about everything he did to our ancestors. That speech. The way he talked about them. The removal of the tribes. It's all so terrible, and we're just going to let him live?"

Moon goes over to a pile of old tires and broken boards and picks up a two-by-four. "I'm going in there to give him what he deserves," she says.

Alice hurries over to try to stop her. "No, leave it alone," she says.

But I can tell Moon is livid. I can see it in her eyes, her heavy breathing, the way she's gripping the two-by-four with both hands.

"Outta my way!" she says, pushing past Alice and running back inside the gas station. I feel compelled to do something, to help calm her nerves and tell her it isn't worth it, so I run after her. Moon shouts at me to stop, but I ignore her and open the back door and go inside.

Inside, I hear Moon banging on the floor with the

94

two-by-four. I turn my phone light on and shine it in her direction.

"Moon!" I yell, but she keeps swinging the two-by-four like a hatchet, knocking it against the floor. Then I see Andrew Jackson scurry away from her and fall through a loose board. Moon slams the two-by-four but misses him. I go over to her and we crouch and hear him scurrying underneath us.

"I think I hit part of his shell," she says, out of breath. "But he still got away. We'll never get him under there."

She tosses the two-by-four and tries to catch her breath. It's justice she desires, a justice that for two hundred years still feels unresolved. I admire her.

"It doesn't matter that he got away," I tell her. "He'll suffer underneath the floor. Or he'll suffocate. Let him live with the vermin and rodents."

She points to the floor. "Look—there's some blood. Maybe I did hurt him."

"Armadillos carry leprosy. You didn't get any blood on you, did you?"

She looks at her hands. "No. Do they really carry leprosy?"

"I've always heard that."

"Gross. Well, if I injured Andrew Jackson and he also has leprosy, then I say justice is served."

We listen for any movement under the floor but don't hear anything. After a moment I help her up and she brushes herself off from all the dust.

"I find such joy in this," she says. "Isn't it fun?"

"You're not even tired," I tell her. "Weren't you afraid of him?"

"That little vermin? Pfff. No way! Let's go tell Alice and Corso what happened."

We use the lights from our phones to find the door and head back outside where Alice and Corso are waiting, but Alice is across the parking lot, peeking over a fence at something.

"What is it?" I call out to her, and look at Corso. "What's happening?"

"We saw someone," he says. "She ran over there before I could stop her."

"You didn't go with her?"

"I—I was about to." Corso looks afraid.

We all watch Alice. It seems she's talking to someone, but it's too dark to see who it is. A shadowy figure.

"We have to help her right now," Moon says. "Ziggy, why don't you go? We'll stay here and make sure Andrew Jackson doesn't get out."

"Me?" I say.

"Yeah, it'll be fine, Ziggy," Moon says.

I start walking across the lot toward the fence. In the darkness I can't see well enough to make out the figure Alice is talking to, so I call out her name and she turns to me.

"Are you okay?" I ask. I feel my anxiety pressing in my chest. I hear a horse and the clopping sounds, like it's trotting away. "Who are you talking to? Who's there?"

"Nobody," Alice says, but something isn't right in the way she answers.

"Was that a horse?"

"Oh," she says, and comes over to me. "Yeah, it was a horse. I tried to pet it but then it ran away."

"Why?"

"I like horses," she tells me. She twists her hair in the moonlight. Alice's eyes almost glow in the night.

"Moon went after the armadillo and chased it under the floorboards," I say. "She got really mad. You should've seen her."

"Well, I'm glad we scared him. He deserves to be chased away after everything he said in that speech. Let's go."

The air feels cooler and still smells of rain. We head back across the lot toward the gas station to Moon and Corso. But when we get there, we don't see them.

Moon and Corso are gone.

(((10)))

Brush Up Your Shakespeare

Where are they?" I shout, looking around.

"Gone," Alice says, very calm. My heart races as we call out for them. At first, I think they're playing a trick, which would be typical of Corso, so full of gags. We used to always play tricks on his dad whenever I spent the night at his house. His dad would fall asleep in a recliner, and while he was snoring we would sneak up on him and tickle his nose with a string until he snapped awake, only to fall right back asleep again.

"Corso, quit playing around!" I call out. "Moon, it's not funny. We have to go! We aren't kidding—we're leaving now!"

I glance around and see the piles of old plywood and boards and used tires. There's a rotted wooden fence that leads to a field behind the station, so I go over to it and see if they're there, but they aren't. Alice goes around one side of the gas station and I take the other side, both of us calling out their names. We meet back in front of the station by Old Hickory Road. I barely have a signal on my phone, so I try calling Moon's phone and Corso's phone, but nobody picks up. I leave messages saying to call us back right away.

"They left us," I say, looking down the road to where we came from. It's too dark to see very far, though, and using the light from my phone doesn't help.

"It'll be fine," Alice says.

"How do you know? This is terrible."

"Well, maybe they decided to go back."

"No—Moon and Corso wouldn't leave like that. You don't think—"

I stop myself because I don't want to say it aloud. Someone kidnapped them and dragged them away. Someone used Andrew Jackson as a decoy to get us off track. Someone has been watching us, or following us out here. But I never heard a car or truck, and I never heard Moon or Corso scream for help when I went to check on Alice talking to the horse.

I look at Alice, who is so composed despite everything that's happening. I'm starting to be freaked out by how calm she is. Just as I start to ask her about it, we see headlights in the distance on Old Hickory Road, bobbing in the dark.

"It must be going slow," I tell Alice. "Still, we should probably hide."

Then we hear the clip-clop of hooves approaching. It sounded just like the sound I heard when Alice was by the fence.

"Oh wow," Alice says, and we see a horse with headlights

around its neck emerge out of the darkness. There's a man on the horse who shouts Alice's name as the horse trots over to us.

"Uncle Gaddith?" Alice shouts back. "Is that you?"

"It is!" he replies. The man pulls the reins and dismounts the horse. He's a stout older man with long gray hair. Alice hurries over to him and they embrace.

"What are you doing out so late at night, Alice?" he asks. "We have to get you home immediately! Don't you know it's dangerous out here?"

"Uncle Gaddith," Alice says, a small nervousness in her voice finally breaking through the calm, "we were on our way to the desert but we've lost our two friends. They've disappeared and we can't find them anywhere."

"Wait," I say to Alice. "Is this the horse you saw a few minutes ago by the fence?"

The horse whinnies and she glances at it. "Nah, different horse."

The man looks out into the darkness and talks loudly. "I knew there was trouble out here. I heard the howl of the Chupacabras. They howl as a warning for me to check the area."

"This is my friend Ziggy—he wants to find his mom," Alice says. "So I'm taking him to explore the desert and maybe find a secret cave or something. But now we've lost his sister and our other friend."

He turns and looks confused. "Are you Ziggy Stardust?"

"It says Ziggy on my birth certificate. My parents were David Bowie fans."

"Fantastic. I'm William Gaddith." The man offers his hand, and we shake. I can feel the tenseness in his grip. "But don't call me William, Bill, Will, or Willie. Just Gaddith."

"Yes, sir."

"Fantastic," he says again. He looks like he could be a knight. His face has the intense, worn look of someone weary from years of hard work. I've seen the same look on my dad's face. His gray hair hangs to his shoulders, and there's a bit of white hair sprouting from his chin.

"It's nice to meet you," I say. I explain to him how my mom disappeared when Moon and I were babies, and how because she loved to explore the desert, I want to see if I can find her in some way. Telling the story quickly like this makes me feel ridiculous and sad, as if I've made the whole thing up, but I can see in his eyes that he holds a great sense of compassion and understanding.

"But why so late at night?" he asks.

"Because it's more fun to explore the desert at night," Alice says, winking at him. Then she nudges him on the arm, like she's keeping a secret from me. I'm not sure why or what it means.

"Well," he says, "we need to find your two friends first, before you look for any cave."

"So what can we do?" I ask.

"Come on—I think I know who can help us tonight." Gaddith motions for us to follow him to the horse. He climbs on and looks down at us.

"This horse is Lampwick," he says. "Say hello, Lampwick."

Lampwick the horse turns its head and looks at us.

"Is he named after the boy in *Pinocchio*?" I ask.

"That's the one," Gaddith says. "But this is really Lampwick. The real Lampwick."

Lampwick turns his head and winks at me. I didn't know horses could wink.

"Get up here," Gaddith says. "Put your foot in the stirrup and climb aboard."

He reaches down to help me. I'm a little afraid of horses, to be honest.

"Okay," I say, and reach up for William Gaddith's hand. I put my foot in the stirrup and he helps me onto the horse. I put my arms around his waist and hang on. Then he reaches and helps Alice up, and she sits behind me.

All three of us are sitting on the horse.

"Are you ready?" he asks us.

"Will the horse buck us off?" I ask back, and he laughs.

"Don't you worry, son," he says. "Just hang on tight, all right?"

I put my arms around him and lean in close. I can feel Alice's arms around me and pressing against my stomach, so we're all nice and tightly snug.

Gaddith kicks the horse into motion, and we trot away, slowly at first. It isn't too bad, but a little bit bumpy. I hear the clip-clopping of hooves against the road. Gaddith kicks again and the horse speeds up, trotting faster until we're galloping.

"Heyaaaaaa, heyaaaa!" he shouts at the horse.

We're suddenly going so fast I can barely hang on from all the hard bouncing as the horse runs. All I can hear is the clomping from the horse and the rumbling of wind in my ears, and I lean into Gaddith's back and hug him harder, closing my eyes and resting my face against his long hair.

"Heyaaaa!" he shouts.

I'm certain I hear Alice laughing behind me, but with all the bouncing and rumbling and clomping, I really don't care—I just want the horse to stop.

"Slow down!" I yell into Gaddith's back, but my voice is too muffled from my face being smashed against him.

"Heyaaaaa!" Gaddith keeps shouting.

We turn down a dirt road somewhere in the desert. I have no idea how far we've traveled out of town. Soon enough—finally!—the horse slows to a trot, and I turn my head to see a vast darkness of desert. In the sky the hazy full moon looks like a white flower glowing in the dark.

We come to an old adobe house. Gaddith leads the horse into the drive and pulls it to a halt.

"Easy does it," he says, climbing off the saddle.

He helps Alice and me off the horse, and as soon as I have both feet on the ground, I fall to my knees and kiss the dirt.

"I thought we would never survive," I tell Alice and her uncle, standing back up.

"What are you talking about?" Alice says. "We were barely trotting the whole time."

"Yes, I went slowly on purpose," Gaddith says. "You really want to go fast, you should ride my motorcycle. We spirits love to ride fast."

"Huh?" I say. "Spirits?"

Gaddith laughs. "Free spirits," he says. "There's no better way to be. Even when you're just a man. A man and his horse, like a cowboy. Except I look like a moron in a cowboy hat."

"Everyone looks like a moron in a cowboy hat," Alice says. "Anyway, look!"

I study the big two-story adobe house in front of us. It's white and brown with some sort of giant satellite on the roof. We can hear opera music coming from inside.

"This is the home of a remarkable Shakespearean actor named Peter O'Doul," Gaddith says. "He's a bit of a recluse and an eccentric, but he knows the desert better than anyone and can surely help us. He worked for NASA once many years ago before acting. These days he owns a winery and tells tall tales."

"What kind of tall tales?" I ask.

"All kinds. He's an equivocator. A prevaricator."

"Huh?"

"A liar. Let me warn you that his overly dramatic Shakespearean speech may be a little difficult to understand, so bear with me."

The adobe house looks like a mansion to me. It sits out here in the desert all by itself, which is a little bit strange but also comforting. We follow Gaddith up the outside concrete stairs that lead to the top floor of the house, where the music is louder.

At the top of the stairs is a large blue door. Gaddith knocks on it three times slowly.

"He only answers to three slow knocks," Gaddith tells us.

"Why?" I ask.

"He has his own way to do everything."

We hear the music turn off inside the house, followed by a roar of laughter. I'm not sure what to expect based on Gaddith's description. To be on the safe side, I take a step to shield myself behind Alice and Gaddith.

A moment later the door flies open and a man in a long robe and slippers answers. He is completely bald and has a big, gray beard. He raises his arms in joy to hug Gaddith.

"Will!"

"O'Doul!"

They embrace and he invites us in. I follow behind my companions, making sure not to make eye contact with him. Whenever my dad gets mad at me, anytime I'm in trouble, he tells me to look him in the eye. Kari might say that's why I don't like confrontation or why I can't look at people of authority in the eye for very long. But I don't think it has anything to do with authority. I simply cannot think straight when I'm looking someone directly in their eyes. It's weird, I know.

"Did we interrupt you?" Gaddith asks Peter O'Doul. "We heard opera playing."

O'Doul pats him on the shoulder and hiccups. He reminds me of an old king or something, with his gray beard and jovial manner.

"Nonsense," he says. "I shall desire you of fair acquaintance, William. This old glabrous fool is lonely this evening. Join me for a feast and a drink in a cup of gaudy gold?"

"Sure," Gaddith says, and he follows O'Doul into the kitchen.

Alice and I look around the room at the tall ceiling and the art on the walls. On one of the walls is a large painting of Venice, Italy. I know because I recognize the gondolas and buildings from pictures we saw in school. On another wall, there are several smaller paintings of ships and buildings and cities. There's a chandelier above us and floor-length drapes at the windows.

"This place is amazing," I say. "Look at those paintings. And that furniture."

"Do you think he's famous?" Alice asks.

"He's definitely rich. This room is bigger than my whole house."

"Uncle Gaddith said he was a Shakespearean actor. In drama class we watched *A Midsummer Night's Dream*, remember? It was funny."

I remember trying to understand *A Midsummer Night's Dream*, but all I could figure out was that it was about a bunch of out-of-control people who drank magic potions and fell in love with each other. And someone turned into a donkey.

Before I can ask Alice about that, Gaddith calls us into the kitchen for pie.

"Did he say *pie*?" Alice asks. "That sounds great—I'm hungry."

I'm not sure I can eat pie while Moon and Corso are missing. There's still no response from them. I guess if Gaddith says O'Doul is our best chance of finding them, I have to believe it. Still, I'm anxious.

We head to the kitchen, which opens to a large dining room. Peter O'Doul invites us to have a seat at the long dining room table. There are candles lit on the table and chairs all around it. I count the chairs—there are five on each side and one at each end. Twelve people can eat at the table! Even the dining room is bigger than my house. A large window overlooks the desert, but it's too dark to see much outside, even with the blue moon. I see my hazy reflection in the window.

"Are you staring at your good looks?" Alice tells me.

"It's so dark out there."

Alice stands next to me and looks into the window—in a smoky haze of darkness, we see our reflections standing there. I wish I could see Moon and Corso out there somewhere. But I can't.

When I turn around, Alice is already sitting at the table, eating her blueberry pie, which Peter O'Doul has placed on the table. I sit across from Alice and watch as he hiccups and fumbles to cut a piece and put it on a saucer for me. He and Gaddith have enormous gold cups they're drinking from that look like chalices. Gaddith sits beside me, and Peter O'Doul sits in front of the blueberry pie.

"I've eaten two pies already tonight," he says happily. "My belly is full, yet I crave more. I'm a man of excess and fun."

"He loves riddles," Gaddith tells us.

"Yes, a riddle," O'Doul says, taking a drink from his gold cup. "O fair Gaddith, I prithee, give me leave to recite a riddle, for being a goodly portly man, I commend a pleasing eye and most noble gesture."

Alice gives me a look, and I know we're both wondering why he's talking in bad Shakespearean English. I want to ask him right away if he can help us find Moon and Corso, but then I remember what Gaddith said about him having his own way of doing things. I sense I need Gaddith to set the stage in order for O'Doul to step out upon it.

"O fair maiden," he continues, "I bid you, be assured I speak not as clown or knave but as noble gentleman. Thou'st come on horseback, ye cuckoo! I am a Shakespearean actor if I were not a rogue or rascal. I played Juliet in my youth, Falstaff in Madrid, and at last, many years later, Bottom in *A Midsummer Night's Dream*. And there sits among us two fair mortals of the land, from land afar methinks, no wild fowl but fair mortals, indeed!"

O'Doul motions his head toward us, but I'm not sure what he's saying. What the heck is he talking about? First, his words are slurring, and second, even if he spoke regular English, I don't think I could understand what he was talking about.

"You mean Natives, like us?" Alice says. "We're Cherokee Nation. All three of us."

"O sweet and gentle Cherokee mortals," O'Doul hiccups. "My soul is in the sky. Tongue, lose thy light. Forgive my ancestors for forcing the Cherokees along the Trail of Tears. They were soldiers, ordered by foolish President Jackson. A weaselly president, indeed."

"Armadillo," Alice corrects.

"Vermin, yes. I pray thee, grant me forgiveness for my ancestors' ignorance and vileness so that I may be relieved of all guilt."

"The first step to forgiveness is to prove you are not, in fact, as ignorant or vile as your ancestors," Alice says. "We do not forget history."

"Yes," O'Doul says, "it is best to remember the Trail of Tears, the removal of Natives from their land. And I thank you for offering the first step to forgiveness."

"Well, we have to learn to forgive," Gaddith says. "I know it's late, but as I was saying earlier about finding Ziggy's sister—"

O'Doul crams a handful of blueberry pie into his mouth and raises a finger. "Think what thou wilt," he says with a mouthful of food, "but methinks I have a great desire to rid myself of a riddle, O mortal youth. My riddle is this: If I recite my poem backward and forward, how will I recite it?"

Alice and I both look at Gaddith. We simply wanted to come in and get help to find Moon and Corso, but now this man is asking us to solve riddles and listen to him read his poems.

"Fine." Gaddith sighs. "Recite your poem for us."

Peter O'Doul stands from the table and closes his eyes. He sways a little and has to steady himself on the back of the chair:

At Roseblood Lake, I sat with a young ghost:
Will Gaddith. He was too afraid to swim
Or play the splashing game. His cousin, Kim,
A lovely girl, was chasing Ben McKee,
While Gaddith, with his birdseed, sat by me.
We lunched that day, a hundred years ago,
With Mrs. Splinter's sixth-grade class. Although
McKee had shared a kiss, I wished him dead,
While Gaddith spoke of spirits. Someone said,
"Look! Kim is chasing Ben!" We heard Ben shout.
And from his mouth a dozen birds flew out!

"It's a lie," Gaddith says into his glass. "I'm no ghost. I am very much alive."

"Never mind all that," Alice says. "The poem is in iambic pentameter. Every other syllable is stressed. Each line has ten syllables."

"Correct," O'Doul says. "A poem of youthful love and ghosts in all its madness, composed in my own avuncular loneliness."

"Madness indeed," Gaddith says, looking at me. "I told you he was a prevaricator, twisting words, bending the truth."

"An equivocator," I say.

"Precisely."

O'Doul sits forward in his chair, his eyes watery. "O fair Moon—where art thou? But what see I? No Moon do we see, alack! Alack!"

I still can't eat my pie, too worried about Moon and Corso.

I ask Gaddith, "Can we leave now and look for them?"

O'Doul crams another handful of pie into his mouth. Blueberry stains are on his robe and bits of blueberry in his beard. For the first time, I sense he is looking at me with sincerity.

"This boy with a full head of hair looks glum," he says.

"We need to find them," I tell him. "They can't be too far away. I'm sure of it."

"I hear the Storyteller is quite the mischievous one," Gaddith says. "I've never seen the Storyteller, but some say it's a spirit who prowls the desert at night. You hear all kinds of strange tales. One involves the Storyteller flying around at night and telling stories. A trickster."

"We were on our way to find a secret cave or some sort of clue to help me find where my mom went," I say. I explain everything, and when I'm finished, O'Doul nods slowly, eyes watery.

"You have bereft me of all words," he says, taking a drink, then wiping his mouth with the back of his hand. "And to this I say thus: On the roof of this mansion sits a fine telescope, good for scouring the deserts or the stars. I beg thee of dearest discretion. It was launched into space, unfolded among water vapors and chlorofluorcarbons. What judgment shall I dread—I am not bound to please thee, but for the sake of gentle Gaddith, sweet and tender hooligan, I forfeit my heart and say thus: Go. Go to the roof and search for your fair sister, Moon!"

Gaddith sets his glass down and motions for us to leave.

"I got it!" Alice suddenly yells, rattling the dishes on the table. "The answer to your riddle—if you recite your poem backward and forward, how do you recite it? Inverse and *in verse*. Right? Am I right, Peter O'Doul?"

I stare in amazement at Alice. I can't believe she was able to figure all that out just from listening to O'Doul recite that poem.

"Gentle and fair maiden hath solved the old riddle," he says. "O vineyards. As the thin and outrageously handsome Rolling Stones sang: 'Thank you for your sweet and bitter fruits.'"

O'Doul drinks the last of his wine, sets his cup down, and belches loudly. Then he reaches into his pie and pinches off more blueberry and tosses it in his mouth. "My feast provoketh the desire."

Alice and I stand from the table, ready to head to the roof.

"And taketh away the performance," O'Doul says, and passes out in his pie.

(((11)))

Mina Minoma,
the Most Pulchritudinous
Fortune-Teller in the Land

Gaddith, Alice, and I take the outside stairs to O'Doul's roof, which is flat and enormous. The nighttime breeze feels good against my face, but I can tell my anxiety is slowly worsening. I try to remember what Kari told me about visualizing my anxiety and realizing it isn't there to hurt me but to protect me. I try to think of it as a protector.

It seems the roof also serves as a balcony for entertainment purposes. There are lounge chairs and small tables. I see a few empty bottles of wine and plastic plates and glasses scattered around like no one ever cleaned up after a party. The telescope is giant and pointing to the sky. It takes all three of us to maneuver it so that it's pointing across the land below us. Gaddith looks through the lens for a long time.

"Well?" we ask him. "What do you see? Is it too dark?"

"This telescope has a built-in light that allows me to see things I've never even imagined," he says, leaning closer into the telescope. "Great Grendel, I can see all the way to Santa Fe. I can see the hard texture of an adobe house. There's an open window and beautiful mauve curtains, silk European bedsheets, a hanging bathrobe with a heart embroidered on the left breast pocket. There are two people kissing . . ."

Gaddith pulls back from the telescope and looks embarrassed. "Never mind, help me move this thing to point in a different direction."

Alice and I help him rotate the telescope to the left so that it points east. Gaddith leans in and looks while Alice and I watch and wait.

"The sharp detail and range of this telescope is impeccable," he says. "It's immaculate. I see coyotes and skunks prowling for food. Tiny lizards scurrying around rocks. Rattlesnakes slithering across the terrain. One has captured a desert rat—uh-oh, the poor thing. I see a lovely snail."

"Uncle Gaddith," Alice says. "What about Moon and Corso? You're supposed to be looking for them."

"Of course, of course. Let me keep looking."

We wait for him, but he can't see anything else. We rotate the telescope to the south, and Gaddith leans in and looks.

"No sign of two kids walking around anywhere. Let's rotate it again."

We rotate the telescope west. I wait. I'm biting my knuckle at this point, worried. I do that sometimes whenever I feel stressed—I bite my knuckle or put my shirt into my mouth and bite on it. I don't know, biting on things seems to ease the anxiety.

"I still don't see them," Gaddith says, and I feel my stomach drop. "But wait—I see Mina Minoma, the most pulchritudinous fortune-teller in the land. She's on the balcony of Casa del Sol. Our troubles are over. She'll be able to help us for sure."

"Pulchritudinous?" I ask.

"Beautiful," he replies. "I dated her once, but I couldn't handle all that beauty."

"What do you mean you couldn't handle it?" I ask.

"I'm worried I'll have a heart attack around her," he says. "She's an angel of beauty. And brilliant and full of visions and delight. She'll be able to find them for sure. Let's go."

We follow Gaddith down the stairs and back to the horse in front of the house. I'm feeling a little bit let down and helpless. Something is not right about this. I was hoping Corso and Moon were playing a trick, but now it's occurring to me that they could be in real danger. Also, it must be after one in the morning by now, and I don't want to think that something terrible has happened to them.

I sit down on the ground after Gaddith and Alice mount the horse.

"Why are you sitting there?" Alice says. "We have to go talk to the fortune-teller."

But I can't bring myself to say anything because I feel myself on the verge of tears. Anytime I get sad, I feel like I need to sit down. Sitting makes me feel better. I put my head down and cry a little. I don't want them to see me crying, but I know they can tell.

"Ziggy," Alice says, in a sympathetic way that makes it worse. Why does that always happen? Anytime I'm crying and someone says my name, it only makes me cry harder. It's embarrassing.

Then she climbs off the horse and comes over to me. She sits beside me and puts her hand on my shoulder. "Hey," she says. "Don't be sad, Ziggy."

But that makes me cry even more. What did my dad call it one time? *Emotional problems.* I have *emotional problems*—that's what he told a teacher once after I panicked about doing a group project in the classroom. It wasn't the project that made me uncomfortable—it was working in the group that day. I don't mind working with other kids or even being in crowds occasionally, but out of the blue sometimes it freaks me out. I'm complicated, I know.

Alice sits with me for a few minutes until I stop crying. Then I lie back, and she lies beside me. Neither of us says anything. The night breeze feels good. We're staring up into the sky, despite Gaddith and the horse waiting on us. The dark sky is my soul, the wind my body. It reminds me of the way Moon and I sometimes lie down on our backs at night in our backyard and gaze up into the sky with an understanding that the earth's beauty is a gift only for us.

A few minutes pass, and soon Alice sits up and turns to me. She doesn't even have to say anything, but I know it's time for us to move on, for me to get myself together and continue our search, so I sit up, too. Here's what my dad would tell me: Don't feel sorry for yourself. To move forward, keep going, and push myself out of my sadness and discomfort. I can hear his voice telling me this. I can hear Kari saying to listen to the sweet Chupacabra telling me he'll be with me the whole time, and not to be afraid. I sense him beside me, wagging his wild Chupacabra tail like an excited dog.

Gaddith is sitting on the horse, stoic as a knight. He smiles as we approach to mount, reaching his hand down to help me onto the horse. Then he kicks us into motion, and quickly we're off again, trotting down the gravel road, listening to the clip-clop of hooves. I'm sitting in the middle again, wedged between Gaddith and Alice, keeping my eyes closed as we gallop forward.

"Heyaaa," Gaddith yells, kicking the horse.

Soon we approach the mountain and start to trot along an uphill path. Finally, I open my eyes, gaze out at the dark desert, and see a house ahead.

"It's the Casa del Sol," Gaddith yells. We come to the gate at the front of the house, and Gaddith pulls the reins and climbs off. He helps me off first, then Alice, and by now I realize my butt is sore from riding that horse so hard.

"My butt is killing me," I tell them.

"You get used to it," Gaddith says. "My ancient butt is hard as concrete. I'm like a statue."

"I think I saw poisonberries along the road when we were riding."

"Poisonberries?"

"They're all over," I say. "You don't have them out here in the desert?"

"I've never even heard of them," Gaddith says. "Are you sure there are poisonous berries?"

"I'm positive! They kill people. Or get them sick. But Moon and I are immune to them."

Gaddith strokes his chin, thinking. "Hmm," he says. "Well, I think we'll all be just fine. And anyway, this is Casa del Sol, House of the Sun, where Mina Minoma lives. See her up there?"

We look up to the balcony and see a woman standing there. She looks tall from down here, almost like a giant. Her hair is long and hangs down past her shoulders. On her shoulder there's a bird we can hear squawking from all the way down here.

"Dear mother of all things majestic, that woman is lovely," Gaddith says. He seems to be in a trance, staring up with his mouth open.

"Uncle William," Alice says, tugging on his sleeve. "Uncle William? Uncle William!"

"Le mot juste," Gaddith says. "What's the exact word to describe such beauty? Is there an exact word in the English language?"

"Pulchritude," I say.

"Precisely. Let's go see her!"

Inside the gate, the gravel trail is lined with small lights and desert plants. We trudge up the trail toward the pink adobe house. As we walk, I see a glistening light coming from the woman. It's like a sparkling star, and it leaves Gaddith transfixed.

"Her jewelry is reflecting the moonlight," Gaddith tells us, breathing hard. He struggles with his breath as we continue to walk. "The woman is crazy about jewelry. She loves to adorn herself. But she's playing tricks on us, trust me. She knows it's me."

"Maybe because she knows you drool all over yourself every time you see her," Alice tells him, which makes me laugh a little, and for a moment I forget about everything we're here for—my sister, my mother, and all things filled with sadness. Walking up the gravel trail is like following an aura of solace and joy in the night breeze. The moon is full in the dark sky, giving everything around us a deep blue haze, dizzy and dreamlike.

By the time we reach the house I feel breathless and as energetic as I've felt all night. "I feel way better," I say. "I'm not feeling sad anymore. Just worried about Moon and Corso."

"The air up here is cool," Gaddith says, looking up to the balcony. "Mina Minoma! We're here to see you to ask for a favor! Are you up there?"

"The steps lead to the giant balcony where she's standing," Alice says. "She just saw us. Surely she's still there."

We take the stone steps that lead to the balcony, a large area with a swimming pool and a table and chairs that overlook the desert below.

Mina Minoma isn't anywhere to be seen.

"She was just here," Alice says.

There's a sliding glass door that leads into the house. We see the light is on and a living room with a couch and chairs, but Mina isn't there either. Gaddith knocks on the sliding door and we wait.

"I don't understand where she could've gone," Alice says.

Gaddith keeps knocking harder and harder. Then we hear a voice from behind us.

"Are you looking for me?"

We turn around and see Mina Minoma standing by the steps we climbed. She's wearing a blue dress and long necklaces that sparkle in the night. Her hair is dark and hangs past her shoulders. She looks stunning, almost statuesque, like a movie star stepping off the screen right in front of us, and I'm as captivated as Gaddith by her beauty. I think of the pictures of my mother, how her hair was similar in its length and color and the way it hung over her shoulder, and I'm suddenly reminded of the simple fact that all I wanted to do tonight was go see my mother. And now here I am somewhere in the middle of the night, in the middle of the desert, outside Poisonberry, trying to find my sister as well. Why did things have to get so complicated and mixed up?

"William Gaddith," Mina Minoma says. "You've come to hear your fortune, I presume?"

Gaddith heads toward her, all smiles. "Sweet pea," he says. "How long has it been?"

"Since you betrayed me? Eleven months, two weeks, and six days, to be precise."

"But my love, my beauty, my sweet pie, my blossom—I wasn't in my right mind. Forgive me?"

We follow Gaddith to Mina Minoma, who crosses her arms and narrows her eyes at him. "I'm not your sweet pea, your sweet pie, or your sweet blossom," she says. "You were a fool, William. No, I take that back. I was a fool to trust you."

She keeps her eyes narrow, staring at him while Alice and I watch. Then she looks at Alice and me as if she's just noticed us.

"Who are these people with you? Children you never told me about?"

Gaddith's face is flushed pink. He's nervous to be around her, I can tell. "This is my niece, Alice, and her friend Ziggy."

Something about Mina Minoma makes me want to reach out and hug her in a tight embrace, in a loving way. Something inside me screams out for her to hold me and tell me everything is going to be fine, that I'll find Moon and Corso and then I'll find my mother, but more than that, it's the feeling of her holding me I realize I'm yearning for.

"Can you help me find my sister and my best friend?" I ask her.

Mina Minoma tilts her head and studies me. "They're missing?"

"Yes. And my mom, too."

"I see," she says. She takes my hand and turns it over so my palm is up. She studies my hand, tracing the lines, lightly touching them. Her finger tickles my hand.

"I see them," she says. Her eyes study my hand. "I see them at a campfire in the desert."

"How do you see them in my hand?"

"Your sister lives in your heart," she says. "You are family, so it's easy."

Alice puts her hand to her mouth in surprise. Gaddith claps his hands. I'm so excited I can barely breathe. "Really? Are they safe?" I ask.

"Yes, they're safe," she says. "They're just down the road from here."

I'm overjoyed, relieved . . . and then immediately I doubt her. After all, I don't really believe in fortune-tellers or people who read palms or anything like that.

"Seriously?" I say. "I want to believe you, but I'm not sure."

Something about Mina Minoma's gaze moves me to completely trust her. I'm drawn by her dark eyes, her motherly smile.

"You have my word," she tells me. "Your sister and your friend are safe."

"What are they doing? Why did they leave?"

She squints into my hand, leans in so close that I can feel her warm breath on my palm. But she shakes her head. "I can't tell. I can only see them sitting by a fire."

"What about my mom?"

Mina Minoma doesn't look at my hand again. She just shakes her head.

Gaddith raises his arms and comes over to hug me. He takes Mina Minoma's hand and kisses it.

Alice has stepped away and she has her back to us. I go over to her and see that she's crying.

"Alice, what's wrong?"

A breeze comes up and blows her hair in her face as she turns to me.

"Ziggy, I lied to you," she tells me. "I have no idea if we can find a secret cave like the one you're looking for. I wanted you to think I knew about a secret place, like I told everyone at school, but I lied about all of it. I thought maybe we could find it . . . but I've never been there before."

She's staring at me, waiting for me to say something, but I can't think of anything to say. I'm not sure I even understand what's happening. My mouth goes dry.

"But there has to be a clue or something where my mom disappeared from out here," I say. "Right? Moon and I both think so."

Alice only stares at me, giving me that familiar look full of sympathy, a look I've become so familiar with my whole life. The look that says: *I feel sorry for you, Ziggy. I'm so sorry, Ziggy.*

I'm not able to say anything else really until Alice reaches for my hand and holds it. Her hand is warm. "I'm sorry I lied to you," she says. "I lied to people at school because I'm different.

We're Cherokee, and people who aren't Native are always saying we look white, like we're lying about being Native. And then we just don't feel like we belong here or at any school."

"Yeah, I get it. So do Bojack-Runt, Sid, Corso, and Sheila. I think we all know what you're saying. But it's okay."

Then we stand there, holding hands, and I feel connected to Alice in a way I haven't before, like she's become my new best friend.

"Are you mad at me, Ziggy? I feel like I led you on. I'm sorry I lied."

"It's okay," I say. "Maybe we can still find a clue about where she disappeared or something. I'm not sure what I'm looking for, really, but there has to be something out here."

"Ziggy, there's something else I need to tell you about me," she says. "I want you to know I'll protect you no matter what."

"Yeah," I say. "You keep saying that. Do you think I can't take care of myself or something? Why are you so worried about protecting me?"

Alice hesitates. "It's because—"

But Gaddith interrupts by calling for Alice, waving for her to go to him.

"I wonder what they're talking about?" Alice asks. "It seems my uncle has a bit of a crush on her. I guess they dated or something. I'll go see what's up."

"Wait," I say. "What were you about to tell me?"

"I'll tell you later. It's not important." She knocks on the screen door, and they let her inside. I turn back to the edge of the balcony overlooking the dark land below and take a deep breath. I'm not sure what to think really. I'm a little bit sad that Alice lied about knowing where to find the secret cave, but then again I'm relieved Moon and Corso are safe.

I think of my mother, wherever she is, and feel somehow like she's watching me. Maybe she can see me right now, staring out into the night, looking up at the stars. Maybe she's in the wind, a spirit flying around watching over Moon and me.

Just then, in the dim light of the front porch, I see a figure move below. I lean over and try to get a better look.

Then I hear a raspy voice: "Ziggy, come down here."

(((12)))

Coyote's Message

The figure moves away before I can see who it is. At first, I wonder if it's Moon or Corso, but the voice was too gruff, too beastly. I step slowly down the stairs and go around to the front of the house where the lights are brighter. There I see it: a coyote. It's Rango, in fact, from earlier tonight, the coyote who thinks he's a Chupacabra.

"Rango?" I say.

Rango prowls over beside the front door where the light is better and looks at me, his eyes red in the night.

"Come here," he says in a hoarse whisper.

I step closer to him so that I can see him well enough in the porch light. He lowers his head and sits. "I have a message for you," he says.

"A message?"

"Do you know the story of the children who were washed up by the sea?"

I shake my head.

"One day many years ago, some children were found washed up on a beach," he says. He speaks in a quiet, low voice as if what he's telling me is the most important secret in the world. "A young girl found them one morning on the beach. They were coughing up the water from their lungs. It was a miracle they survived. Nobody knew who they were and the only language they spoke was Cherokee, and the young girl who found them was Cherokee also."

"I don't understand," I tell him. "Why are you telling me this?"

Rango's eyes glow red in the night. "Because the children said they arrived from two hundred years ago, and they couldn't go back to the past. The young girl told them she would protect them, so they followed her to her family, who lived in underground tunnels. The girl and her family were immortal Nunnehi, Cherokee spirits who give protection."

"Why didn't the children go back to the past?"

"They couldn't. They weren't really from the past. They believed that, but deep down they knew it wasn't true. You can't go back to the past, Ziggy."

"The Nunnehi captured them and kept them underground?"

"No, the Nunnehi protected them. Even though they thought they were from the past, they were just orphaned children, so soon they lived with the Nunnehi."

I think about what he's telling me, but I'm not sure why he's telling me this. And why he's come all the way out here in the desert to tell me. The sky above us is dark with the moon glowing somewhere way out there in the middle of space, like a floating and lost light. Does the moon understand its impact on everyone down here on Earth as we gaze up at it as if to ask it some unanswerable question? Does the moon even recognize how important it is to the world and science and the universe?

Then I think, maybe we're all lost lights, too, like the moon, unsure of our existence, why we're here and whatever we're supposed to be doing.

Rango's tongue is hanging from his mouth as he pants. "The Nunnehi are closer to you than you think," he says. Then he starts to walk away, his tail hanging low.

"Wait!" I say. "Why are you telling me this now? Is someone a Nunnehi here? Are you?"

But Rango has already slinked away into the darkness.

Back upstairs, inside the house, Mina Minoma hands me a cup of tea. "Drink this," she says. "It's a special tea to keep you awake."

Alice takes a sip from her cup and says she herself was getting sleepy. "It hit me all of a sudden," she says. "I couldn't keep my eyes open, so Mina made us tea."

Mina's house is full of books and colored vases. There are red vases and green vases on one wall, and on another wall are blue and yellow vases. Her walls are stone and there's a fireplace in the corner of the room with a sleeping cat lying on a rug in front of it.

"My cat's name is Maceo," Mina says. "Named him after the Jane's Addiction song. But he thinks he's a human, always locking me out of the upstairs bathroom and hogging the toilet. You should see him with a fork and spoon at the dinner table."

"I've known plenty of animals who may as well be human," Gaddith says, winking at me.

"Or plenty of humans who may as well be animals," Mina adds, nudging Alice. "Look at your uncle here. He's a big, ridiculous, goofy yeti. When he was first in love with me, instead of calling me on the phone he would step outside his house and moan in lovesick pain until I turned on my outside light to signal I could hear him. I fell in love with him, too."

Gaddith takes a bow. "As Shakespeare says, 'The course of true love never did run smooth.'"

He and Mina gaze into each other's eyes as if they're suddenly under some strange potion of love, some magic that the lines from *A Midsummer Night's Dream* just ignited.

"Awkward," Alice says, motioning for us to go outside.

I follow her back outside to the balcony and close the door behind me. We hear music start from inside and see Mina throw her arms around Gaddith's neck. They begin slow dancing.

"Definitely awkward," I say. "And anyway, this isn't the time to be slow dancing."

Alice is staring at me, and I can feel my face flush, so I turn away from her.

"Why are you so shy, Ziggy?" she asks.

I don't say anything. I have a strange premonition that Alice wants me to look at her, but I can't make eye contact, can't bring myself to even try to understand what's happening.

I move over to the edge of the balcony and tell her the story Rango told me.

"He was here?" she says. "How did he find us here?"

"I don't know."

"Are you sure it was him?"

"I'm positive. I think? He's a coyote and they all look alike to me."

She's staring at me again. "So, did he tell you a Nunnehi was protecting you?"

"No."

"Didn't you pay attention to his story?"

"Yeah, but I don't get what you're saying. What am I missing?"

Alice shakes her head, frustrated, but I don't get why she's acting like that. Just then we hear the sliding door open, and Gaddith and Mina come out holding hands.

"We have an announcement to make," Gaddith says.

Alice and I look at each other.

"We're in love!" he says.

Alice says, "You're *what*?"

"We're in love," Mina says. "There's a kind of magic about falling in love I can't really explain. You just have to experience it. But I've realized I've always been in love with William Gaddith."

Alice hugs Gaddith and Mina, and I shake their hands because hugging makes me uncomfortable. Everyone seems very happy, but I have to remind them about why we're here.

"Can we go find Moon and Corso now?" I say, and Mina looks into my hand again.

"I just want to make sure they're still down the road," she says, but then I see her face go serious. She puts a hand to her mouth. "Oh no," she says.

"What?" I ask. "What is it? Is something wrong?"

"They're gone," she says.

(((13)))

Bela Lugosi Is Dead

Mina spends the next ten minutes looking into both of my hands, but she can't find anything. "Nothing is showing up," she says.

"What does that mean?" Alice says. "We should've gone the moment you saw them earlier."

We all fall silent, thinking.

"Maybe we should just go looking for them again," I say. "It's dark out there, but if we yell loudly enough, maybe they'll hear us."

"I have another idea," Mina finally says. "Come with me, everyone."

We follow her inside the house and down the hallway to a room lit by an oil lamp. The room has a kind of bewildering, empty appearance, with only a large standing mirror and a small box set in the middle of the floor. Our shadows flicker across the bare walls as we enter. The room feels draftier, too, as if there's an open window, but there are no windows.

"Our only hope is to entertain my wise old snake, Bela Lugosi, and hope he can tell us where Moon and Corso are," Mina explains.

"Bela Lugosi is dead," Gaddith says.

"Who's he?" Alice asks.

"A famous silent movie star who played Dracula," Gaddith tells us. "If you've seen those old black-and-white silent movies with Dracula, that's Bela Lugosi."

"He's a very wise, old, prophetic snake," Mina says, "and he's inside that box."

We all look at the box. I feel a chill along my spine.

"A snake?" I say. "I don't like snakes."

"Me neither," Alice says, leaning into me. She takes my hand and holds it, which is awkward, but I like how warm her hand is, and somehow it makes me feel better.

"Why don't you like snakes?" Mina asks.

"They're creepy and they attack," I tell her.

"They gross him out," Alice adds. "I mean, snakes bite, right?"

"So do dogs," Mina replies. "And you like dogs, don't you?"

I look down at the floor, try to make sense of her logic, but somehow it doesn't make me feel any better. "Yeah, I like dogs, but snakes crawl on their bellies."

"So do dogs."

I think again. "Well, snakes stick out their tongues."

"So do dogs."

She's right, but I'm still worried.

Mina places a hand to her chin, as if deep in thought. "We have to tell Bela Lugosi a story."

"What kind of story?" Alice asks.

"Anything, really. If he likes it, he'll help us. But if he doesn't like it, he'll spit a green fluid."

"Venom!" Alice and I say at the same time.

Mina laughs. "It's not venom. It's not poisonous. It's just green saliva."

"Green spit?" I say.

Gaddith clears his throat loudly and holds up a finger. "I have a snake phobia, too," he says. "Do you still find me attractive, my love? My sweet pea?"

Mina smirks at him and steps over to the box.

I'm not sure what to think. The thought of knowing a snake is inside the box is terrifying. I once saw a snake on a hike near our house, and I had nightmares for months afterward. My dad kept telling me snakes aren't necessarily bad, they just have survival mechanisms like all other creatures. My therapist, Kari, once had me watch YouTube videos of snakes so I would desensitize to them. I spent an hour every day for a whole summer watching videos of snakes slithering across the ground, and for a while the nightmares continued, but then they stopped suddenly, and it didn't bother me anymore. I could watch videos of snakes without it bothering me or giving me anxiety.

Still, knowing a live snake is in the box is unnerving.

"Bela Lugosi," Mina says to the box, tapping on top of it with a finger. "Are you awake? We have visitors. Can you come out and see them?"

Alice and I step behind Gaddith, whose hands are trembling at his side as Mina taps again on the box.

"Bela Lugosi," she says, crouching down. "Come out this instant, do you hear me?"

The snake rises out of the hole in the box, stretching his long neck until he is eye to eye with Mina. Gaddith lets out a quiet whimper. The snake's eyes are dark and focused directly on Mina. Then he turns his head to us and opens his mouth, revealing sharp teeth and a small, flickering tongue.

"Tell me a *story*," the snake hisses.

"If we tell you a story," Mina says, "will you tell us where two children are right now?"

The snake is swaying. "*Yesssss. If the story is good.*"

Before anyone can stop him, Gaddith steps forward and tells the snake exactly how we ended up there in the middle of the night, and that he was in love with Mina.

Immediately, the snake opens his mouth and spews a green liquid in Gaddith's face, which makes Gaddith shriek.

"It's poison!" he cries out. "Help me!"

"You're fine," Mina assures him. "I told you—it's not poison, it's snake saliva, which unfortunately is green and stains clothes and carpet, so try not to get it on any of my rugs."

The snake is looking at me, and Alice speaks up. "Someone

here has a story," she says. "The world is full of stories. Sad stories, happy stories, scary stories. You have stories of your family. Funny stories, strange stories. That's how we learn best, through storytelling."

Alice whispers to me. "Think of a Cherokee story—quick!"

"I can't," I whisper back. "Too scary. I can't think."

"Yes, you can," she tells me. "It's fine. You can do it. Think of a Cherokee story your grandma told you."

"I've gone blank."

"You've gone blank? What does that even mean? You can't think?"

"I've gone blank."

"Take a deep breath," she tells me. "This is totally not a big deal."

My heart is racing, not so much from the thought of the snake spitting on me, but how I can't think in times of pressure like this, almost always. But then I think: How did Alice know my grandma told us stories? Did I mention that to her? Did Moon say something earlier in the night? How could she possibly have known that?

"All right," Alice says to the snake. "I have a story about protectors."

The snake lowers his head and narrows his red eyes at her. "Protectors?"

"The spirits who protect our people."

"Pro*ceed*," he hisses.

"A very old man was certain that the world was ending

because it rained and flooded every night," Alice says. "The storms brought high winds and a hard rain thrumming against his window. Outside, the tips of the highest trees waved and lost leaves and branches. And the old man worried. He worried about falling ill, too, he worried he never had enough money, and he worried he was dying soon. Better to stay inside and stay well. Better to avoid people. The town recluse, they called him, because he never left the same rickety gray house he had lived in for sixty years.

"Then one day while he was working in his garden, he saw a young girl peek her head over the fence he had built around his yard. *I'm here to protect you*, she told him. *You don't need to worry about dying because you will live to be over one hundred years old. And no storm or sickness will hurt you.* But the old man did not believe her. He told her to go away and leave him alone.

"Late that night it rained, and the old man heard someone outside calling his name. He looked out the window and saw a woman across the road calling to him for help, so the old man put on his raincoat, grabbed his umbrella, and went outside to help her. When he got outside, the rain had let up to a sprinkle, and he headed across the road where the woman was, but he couldn't find her. He heard drumming coming from a clearing inside the woods and saw a light, which he walked toward. When he got to the clearing, he found the little girl and her family singing and dancing and playing music. The family welcomed the old man, gave him food and drink, and let him enjoy their music until the sun began to rise.

"When the old man arrived back home, he saw great clouds of dark smoke billowing from his house. His house had been on fire. There were firefighters who told him he was lucky he had escaped the fire. It was then the old man realized the girl and her family had rescued him. He went back to the clearing to find them, but they weren't there. When he was a child, he had heard stories about the immortal beings who protected the Cherokee. He knew the girl was his protector."

Bela Lugosi lowers his head and flickers his tongue, but he doesn't spit. "Well," he hisses, "that story is *fine*, but it's not believable."

"Stories don't have to be believable to be true," Alice tells him.

"And stories don't have to be true to be believable," Gaddith adds. "But I know for a fact that Alice's story is true because I was there. I saw the Nunnehi dance and play their music."

I'm surprised Gaddith says this, which must certainly be a lie, but he looks serious.

The snake narrows his eyes. "See, now I *know* you're rattling my rattler. But it's still not good enough. I need a better story."

Alice nudges me, motioning for me to go.

"I guess I can tell him the story of the Snake Man," I whisper, and she nods, pushing me forward so that I step closer to Bela Lugosi.

Mina motions me to come even closer, telling me it's fine. "Bela won't hurt you," she promises.

I take a deep breath. I can't believe I'm allowing myself to do this, but I take a few steps so that I'm standing beside Mina and looking at Bela Lugosi.

The snake stares at me. His head is swaying. His tiny red tongue flickers.

"*Proceed* with your story," he hisses.

"Once upon a time," I say, "two hunters went into the woods together to hunt. One hunter was not successful in killing anything, but the stronger, taller hunter killed a rabbit and several squirrels. When evening came, they lit a fire to prepare their supper. The taller hunter showed the dead squirrels but hid the rabbit so he could eat it all himself. The other hunter warned him that if they ate squirrel meat, they would become snakes. The taller hunter laughed and didn't believe him. He went on with roasting the squirrels and rabbit and ate them while the other hunter fell asleep by the fire. Late that night, the hunter who didn't eat heard the taller hunter moaning in agony, twisting his body. The hungry hunter sat up and saw the lower part of the tall hunter's body had already changed to the body and tail of a giant snake. The tall hunter moaned and wailed for help, so the other hunter tried to calm him but could do nothing else. The tall hunter's skin turned scaly until at last even his head was a serpent's head. The hungry hunter became very afraid of his companion, but the tall hunter slithered away from the fire and down the bank into the river."

I'm ready to cover my face and fall to the floor, but instead of spitting at me, the snake turns and spews a green liquid across the room that hits Gaddith right in the face.

Gaddith shrieks.

"Poisoned again!" he yells. "I'm dying. Great Grendel—my eyes! I'm going blind!"

"Relax," Mina tells him, rushing over to help him with his shirt as they wipe the green goo from his face. "Stay here, I'll go get a towel."

Mina leaves the room and I see the snake's head swaying back and forth. Now he's looking at me again, but I'm worried he'll spit the green liquid at me, so I step back.

"Don't be *afraid*," the snake hisses. "Your story has great *meaning*. Do you *know* what it means?"

I shake my head. "It's just a story my grandma used to tell."

"The tall hunter was selfish," Alice speaks up.

"That is *correct*," the snake hisses. "But he *also* did not bite his *companion*. Even a *snake* can be a friend."

Gaddith comes over beside me, his face dripping with green goo. "Wait a minute. If a snake can be a friend, and if you liked the story, why did you spit on me?"

"Because even a *snake* can have a sense of humor," the snake replies, and opens his mouth and spits into Gaddith's face again.

Gaddith cowers, shivering. "Nooo!"

The snake lowers himself back into the hole in the box.

Mina returns to the room with a towel and helps Gaddith clean up. "He's a trickster," she says. "A typical snake. But as I said, he's harmless."

Gaddith's eyes are bloodshot from the spit. "He's hardly

harmless," he says, blinking rapidly. "And what about the prophecy anyway? What about telling us where the two kids are?"

Mina turns and sees Bela Lugosi has hidden himself back inside the box. "Not so fast," she says, tapping on its top. "Bela, you owe us. Come on."

The snake slowly rises, and this time Alice, Gaddith, and I all shield our faces. Mina crosses her arms and looks at the snake, who sways and flickers his tongue.

"I *see* that you won't let me *sleep*," the snake hisses, "so I'll *give* you what you want. *Bring* me the crystal."

"I have it right here," Mina says, pulling from her pocket a small, oval blue stone that sparkles in the dim room. She sets it down on the box, and the snake stares directly into it, still swaying.

"I *see*," he hisses. "Yes. A boy and a girl *standing* at the *edge* of the mountain. The stars show the *west* side of the mountain."

"Thank you, Bela," Mina says, touching him lightly on the head.

"Bring me a *rat* and I'll *behave*," the snake says, lowering himself into the box.

Alice looks horrified. I'm positive I look afraid, too.

"Let's go," she says. "We should hurry before it's too late."

"Too late for what?" I ask.

"Who knows? Anything's possible tonight, it seems."

I follow her and Gaddith back outside to Mina's balcony, where Mina bids us farewell.

We thank her, and she throws her arms around Gaddith's

neck and kisses him, which embarrasses me so badly I can feel my face flush.

From the top of the stairs, looking out into the darkness toward the Organ Mountains, I can see a tiny orange light flashing.

It must be Moon.

(((14)))

The Raven Mockers

Heyaaa!" Gaddith yells, kicking Lampwick into motion.

Off we ride, east toward the mountains. I hear the clip-clop of hooves against the ground and feel the jarring bounce as I squeeze Gaddith's waist. This time I keep my eyes open. We're moving faster than ever, the horse galloping at full speed and the cool desert wind in my face.

"I see a light up ahead!" Gaddith calls out to us.

I can't see anything ahead of us since he's taller than me, and trying to lean over and look over his shoulder could be fatal, so I keep holding on and thinking how riding a horse isn't really as bad as I thought. You would've never gotten me on a horse before this night, but now that I've done it a few times, I could see myself doing it again.

Soon, Gaddith pulls the reins, and we slow to a trot. Ahead, I see the orange light of a fire, but it's too dark to see anything else. I can smell the smoke from the flames, stronger as we get closer. Gaddith stops the horse, and I hear Moon call out to us:

"You found us! Come in here!"

We see Moon and Corso disappear into an opening in the mountain. While Gaddith helps Alice and me down, I call out for Moon but she doesn't respond.

"They ran into an opening," I say.

"Amazing," Gaddith says. "I've never seen it. But the light of the fire helps."

We move closer to the opening in the mountain, which reveals a yellow light inside. I call out again, this time to both Moon and Corso. Then Alice calls for them.

"What do we do?" I ask. "Go in? Maybe they found a clue or something."

Alice looks worried, and I'm guessing it's guilt she is feeling for lying to me about a secret cave, but here we are, and it feels real.

"I'm getting bad vibes," she says.

"Maybe it's a secret mountain instead of a secret cave," I tell her. "Maybe it *is* real after all."

She isn't convinced, and neither is Gaddith, who is stroking his chin and thinking. "Well, we have to go inside and see," he finally says. "They just went in there."

The mountain opening is narrow and maybe seven or eight feet high. There's a light flashing inside, so I know it's lit. We enter the opening and follow the tunnel, with Gaddith leading the way. Alice follows him with her hand on his arm, and I follow Alice, holding her arm.

Torches are lit along the walls on both sides. The tunnel is cool and hollow. We hear the odd echo of dripping water followed by the echo of Moon's laughter from somewhere ahead. I want to call out to her, but I'm too afraid.

"It's creepy in here," I tell Alice and Gaddith.

"We'll be fine," Gaddith says, but something in his voice tells me he isn't so sure either.

"Don't worry, we'll protect you," Alice tells me.

Our shadows flicker along the wall from the torchlight. The ground is mostly gravel and dirt, and we walk slowly, as quietly as possible, down a long tunnel that winds around until I see Moon and Corso. I immediately run over to Moon and hug her.

"You guys found us," she says. "What took you so long?"

"What took us so long?" I say. "We thought you guys were kidnapped or dead. We were scared to death."

Corso comes over and hugs me, too. Even though I've always felt awkward about hugging, tonight I'm feeling like I actually kind of like it.

Alice introduces them to Gaddith, who bows and says, "My pleasure to meet you both. We're so relieved you're safe."

"They told us you would find us," Moon says. "The people down at the end of this tunnel. They told us to wait here by the fire with you."

"The people?" Alice asks. "What people?"

"They told us they're our protectors."

Alice and Gaddith look at each other like they know something the rest of us don't. Moon notices it also and asks, "What is it?"

"Never mind," Gaddith says.

"This must be a secret mountain," Corso speaks up. "That's what we're thinking, because the people told us they have secrets to tell us."

"But why did you leave us when we were at the gas station earlier?" I ask.

"I didn't think it was a good idea at first," Moon says, "but then this old man and woman came right up to us and asked what we were up to, so we told them we were looking for clues to find Mom. That's when they became super friendly and told us they had wild parsnip back here that would help us. They seemed harmless and said they would drive us here and then return us if you weren't coming."

Corso adds, "They said the stars were aligned perfectly so that you would be here soon, and here you are. They build a fire to cook their meat outside."

"Oh no, no, no," Alice says, leaning into Gaddith, who starts to comfort her. "Please tell us you didn't eat it."

"The meat is bad," Gaddith says. "Did they tell you what it is?"

"No," Corso says. "Just that it's heart. It sounds gross. Who eats heart?"

"The Raven Mockers," Alice says. "You know the stories

146

about them, right? Did your grandma tell you the story when you were little?"

"Oh, the Raven Mockers," Moon says, and looks at me. "Remember, Ziggy? Grandma told us a story about the Raven Mockers?"

"Oh, I remember that story. There was a boy who pretended to be sick so he wouldn't have to go to school. All day, every day, the boy ate candy instead of going to school. He ate so much candy and never went anywhere, so he got fat. One night as the boy was falling asleep, a witch flew just like a raven to his house and snuck in through his window. While the boy was sleeping, the witch ripped his heart out with her claws and ate it."

"Those stories can be scary," Alice says. "When the Raven Mockers can't find people, they change form to humans, but they always look old because they've ripped out and eaten so many hearts in the past. We have to get out of here."

"I can't believe it," Moon says, looking at Corso. "Did they really trick us here?"

"They seemed so nice," Corso says.

"And sweet. Plus there's the perpetual fire burning outside, which I thought confirmed our protectors would arrive soon."

Just then Gaddith motions for us to be quiet. We watch him and listen. We can hear the sound of a howling wind like on a cold winter night.

"Sounds like ghosts," Alice says quietly. "That's the sound the Raven Mockers make. We need to leave."

Moon and Corso aren't convinced, though. "We have to talk to them and make sure," Moon says.

"We shouldn't," Alice tells her. "It's really not safe being here."

Moon ignores her and hurries off. "Follow me."

I'm not sure whether to believe Alice or Moon. Everything feels so strange and dreamlike, and all I wanted to do was explore caves safely for clues about my mom's disappearance. The inside of this mountain feels creepy and unsafe, but I try to ignore it.

We trail behind Moon, stepping quietly like hunters, along the winding path until we reach the end of the tunnel, where an old man and woman are sitting on the ground, eating meat that smells sweet and delicious.

They look up at us as we approach, but they don't speak or stop eating. The man is wearing a black coat and dark hat. The old woman is wearing a long, dark dress that looks like it's from the 1800s.

Alice leans in close to me. "They're the Raven Mockers," she whispers. "They disguise themselves to lure people. We have to be careful."

The old man looks up and stares at us with dark eyes and sagging jowls. He motions for us to approach, but nobody moves.

"You're trying to find your mother," he tells us. "Do you want to find her tonight?"

"Is it really possible?" Moon asks. She looks at me to speak up, but I remain quiet.

The old woman bursts into laughter, spewing bits of food from her mouth. She's reclined against the wall, a whole mess of food on her belly.

"What's so funny?" Moon asks. "I don't understand what's happening."

The old man stands. He is long faced and of crooked posture. "I have bad news," he says. "You will never find your mother. Not tonight, not ever, unless you do something for me."

"It's a trick," Gaddith warns. "Don't listen to him."

"Look," the old man says, pointing to the wall. "Bloody mouth, dead head. Do not leave or you'll be robbed of all your memories of your mother. Your mouth will bleed all the memories out of your head, and they'll be gone forever."

My heart is racing. The way he talks, his low, creepy voice, makes my anxiety rise.

"They won't fall for your tricks," Alice says.

The old man motions for us to come closer. "Eat parsnip here, which will cure you from losing your memories of your mother." He looks at me and takes a step forward. "You, especially you. Let me say right now that you'll be so confused whenever people ask you about your mother that they will begin to label you—and it will happen a lot—as having brain problems so often that you'll end up hating yourself. You'll be so distressed that you'll wonder why it all had to happen to you. Are you listening, hmm?"

But I don't understand what he's talking about.

His eyes narrow as he stares at me. "Let me explain

something. For a while you'll learn to dismiss what others think, even though on the inside you'll know they're right because you've already examined how deeply troubled you are. And this will happen over a long period of time, through various counselors and psychologists and even psychiatrists who'll give you medication. For a long time you won't be able to make any sort of oral testimony about any of this or your mother with anyone—not friends, not family, not even loved ones. But if you eat the parsnip, your memory will grow even more, and you'll have even more memories of your mother. Do you understand what I'm saying? Come here and eat."

"He's not falling for that," Gaddith tells him with a stern voice. Alice takes a step in front of me and stares at the old man until he takes a step back.

"Sit down," she tells him.

Then Gaddith yells, "Run!"

We all turn and run as hard as we can back through the tunnel. My heart is racing so fast I can barely breathe as I run ahead of the others. We hear a loud screech, and as we stop and turn around, we don't see the man and woman, but two large ravens. Alice was correct—Raven Mockers! Now they're coming after us.

We all run back to the entrance. As soon as I make it back outside, I run to the horse and turn to see the others, thankfully, right behind me.

"Take the horse to my house!" Gaddith yells at us. "I'll get them to chase me the other way!"

Alice immediately mounts the horse and helps me up. Then we help Moon and Corso climb behind us, right as I see the clumsy birds emerge from the opening in the mountain. Gaddith makes himself super visible under the moon, and the ravens turn and follow him as he runs away into the night.

(((15)))

Jean-Pierre,
the Opera-Singing Frog

We take off with a jolt. Lampwick breaks into a gallop while we all hang on for our lives, moving through the dark desert. I can hear Corso and Moon screaming behind me as we ride through cacti and plants, eventually making it to a gravel path where Alice pulls the reins to slow Lampwick to a trot.

Through a chill, with a shudder of delight, I feel a kind of drowsy calm. The sky above us is dark and gloomy, absent of brooding clouds. The land around us is composed of strange, shadowy plant shapes.

"Do you know where we are?" I ask.

"No!" Alice calls back.

"I think we're safe now!"

She pulls Lampwick to a stop and I let out a deep breath. "That was terrifying," I say.

"Help me down!" Corso yells. I'm glad this time I'm not the only one eager to get off the horse.

Alice dismounts first, then helps me down. We both reach and help Moon and Corso climb off. Corso falls to his knees and kisses the ground.

"They were Raven Mockers," I say. "Alice, you were right."

"We didn't know," Moon swears. "They seemed so caring at first."

I look up and see the stars swirling in the sky, blinking. The sky is vast and dark and full of stars up there. I must be staring, because Moon touches my arm and asks me what's the matter.

I look at her. "It's just that I don't think we'll find anything tonight to help us locate where Mom disappeared."

"Why do you say that?"

"It's so late." I feel exhausted and take a deep breath. "And we've spent all this time just looking for you two. Maybe we should call it quits and hope we can come back and find a clue or something on another night."

"Ziggy," Alice says. "The Sun became sad, too, remember, after her daughter died in the Ghost country, the Darkening land in the west. Do you know that story?"

I shake my head.

"The Sun never smiled and hid from the Earth because she was so sad. But a drummer entertained her by beating the drum and singing, and then others played music and danced, and she rose in the east and shone again."

Corso says, "The band's not here, so we can't cheer you up that way."

Alice looks up to the stars and something changes in her face, as if she sees something up there. In the darkness all around us, the desert plants and cacti look crooked, as if they are etched with worry and fear, and in the distance I can see the moonlight embracing the sky as its own, Mother Moon and all her swirling little stars, her children.

"It's been a strange night," I say, and look down to see an insect twitching in the dirt. I kneel down and pick it up, but it stops moving, and I wonder if it has died in my hand.

Just then we hear a rustle in the darkness, and a reddish-brown hawk steps out of the desert and stands before us in the road, lifting its wings.

"It's a hawk," Moon says, taking a step back and grabbing my arm.

The hawk lowers its wings, and we see two other hawks step up behind it. All three hawks seem to be watching us.

"What do you want?" Alice calls out.

"We're just drifters," one of the hawks says. "My name is Agiyosi."

"Agiyosi," Alice says. "That means 'I am hungry' in Cherokee. Are you looking for food? I thought hawks only come out in the daylight."

The hawk's eyes glow red in the night. "The best food is found at night. I have dismantled desert rats, snakes, and mice all in one night by swooping down on these paths. My eyesight is better than humans'. But tonight there is nothing. They're all hiding, I suspect, from your noises."

"We don't have any food," Alice tells the hawk.

The hawk lowers his head. "It's just as well. I'm full of stories but empty of food. If you see any mice or snakes, whistle loudly and I'll come."

"If you tell us a story," Alice says, "I'll bring you plenty of food tomorrow night. We have a shed full of mice."

"I'll trust you," the hawk says. "But all my stories are sad, like bad music. Once upon a time, my grandmother lived alone. She was a very lonely woman. The end."

We wait for the hawk to continue.

"That was pretty bad," Alice calls out. "That's the whole story? That's it?"

"I'm weak with hunger," the hawk says, "but I'll continue since I trust you will bring me food. I'm as hungry as a walrus. Goo goo g'joob."

"He's a John Lennon fan," Corso says happily.

We all shush him so we can hear the hawk continue:

"My grandmother," he goes on, "was lonely as any person whose husband had left in the first year of marriage out of regret and fear, claiming he had made a terrible mistake by rushing into a lifelong commitment. He was such a coward—a weak, cold coward."

"Your grandfather?" Moon asks.

The hawk cocks his head and flutters his wings. "Yes, my pitiful grandfather. And my grandmother used to say, 'Let him

155

run back to his mother like a frightened baby bird after eight months away from her. Go away, you sad bird, go back to your mama.' She never wanted to see him or talk to him again. And during this time of her misery and loneliness, whenever the growling of bears or the snapping of twigs caused a panic, she realized she was not quite herself anymore. She spent whole afternoons in seclusion. She picked up rice in churches, like Eleanor Rigby. She tried killing rats and using their blood to paint on rocks, but she felt no inspiration. Her dreams were filled with cobbled streets and old buildings with deteriorating structures and broken windows, images of sadness and destruction. But then she realized she can't change the past. What happened is done. She learned to forgive him, and she became a strong and resilient hawk."

The hawk then turns and flies with its two companions into the darkness.

"Weird. I never knew hawks were so smart," Moon says.

"I never knew they could talk," Corso tells her.

We agree it is strange, and Alice points out its purpose. "The point of the story is that the hawk's grandmother accepted what had happened to her, right? Do you see that, Ziggy?"

"Yeah, I guess," I say, but truthfully, I don't care what the hawk had to say. I want to find Gaddith. "We should find your uncle. I'm worried about the Raven Mockers. I hope he got away."

I pull out my phone and turn on the light. "Alice, what's his address? Maybe we can use GPS."

"I don't have a signal," she says.

I see that I don't have one either.

"That's why I couldn't text you earlier," Moon says. "We couldn't get a signal at all. So what do we do now?"

We all have our phone lights shining. Corso walks over to the side of the road and stares at something. "Hear that?"

We fall silent and listen, but we can't hear anything. My phone shows it's 4:57.

"It's almost five in the morning!" I whisper. I don't think I've ever been up this late.

Corso puts a finger to his lips for me to be quiet. It's so dark out here I'm afraid we won't be able to find our way anywhere until sunrise. He flashes the light from his phone toward the cacti and desert. I look around for poisonberries and see a few along the trail.

"Watch out for the poisonberries," I warn him.

He says, "I could've sworn I heard a frog."

"In the desert?"

"There are desert toads," Moon says. "They sleep under rocks during the day and come out at night, so it's possible. But my question is: Who cares? We need to get out of here."

"Exactly," Alice says. "But which way? We need to figure it out quick."

A large frog hops out of the darkness and onto the road. Startled, we all shine our phone lights at him.

"I knew it!" Corso says. "See? A frog. A desert toad, or whatever."

The frog's eyes blink. "Bon soir," he croaks. "I am yours if you want to fall in love. Kiss me and watch me grow back into the man I once was back when I wore a German fedora hat and auctioned Venetian paintings in Europe as a side gig while my opera career developed."

Alice, Moon, Corso, and I all look at each other.

The frog stands on his hind legs and bows. "I am Jean-Pierre Le Peu, famous operatic baritone. Er, excusez-moi, *former* opera star, I should say, back when I was still a man. I'm looking for a way to destroy the spell put on me. Will you kiss me and see if the spell dies, mon amour?"

"Kiss you?" Moon says. "Absolutely not."

Jean-Pierre looks at Alice, blinks.

"No offense, but I'm not kissing you either," she says.

Jean-Pierre's shoulders slump. "It is just as well. I'll never be able to return to the nineteenth century anyway. Oh, it is too sad—I'll never be able to sing again."

"You can't return to the past," Alice tells him. "Didn't you just hear the hawk's story? You have to learn to keep moving forward. And you better watch out—he may try to eat you."

"The hawks aren't interested in me," Jean-Pierre croaks. "They're too busy dismantling their desert mice and rats. What are you doing out here in the middle of the night?"

Moon tells him about our mom.

Jean-Pierre's eyes are big and filled with tears. "That is sad. I'm learning that the only help I get is from myself." He blinks, looking around at all of us. It occurs to me that his life is terrible, being a frog when he was once a person. He's right out of a fairy tale. "Look at me," he croaks. He points to the top of his head. "The two yellow marks up there? You know the story about how I got them?"

"I know that story," Alice says. "It's an old story. The bullfrog lost a bet to a gambler after losing a game."

"It's a bunch of bull," the frog croaks. "The real story is I had a yellowbird paint them on my head to win the love of a beauty who sadly refused my efforts. It doesn't matter."

He hops over between Moon and Alice and stares bulging-eyed at them. "Where have you two been all my life?"

Moon and Alice both step away from him.

Jean-Pierre's tongue flies out and catches a mosquito, which he quickly swallows. "Is it my halitosis?"

"What?" Alice says. "No. You're a frog. And anyway, we have to go. We really appreciate everything you've done."

"Before you go," he croaks, "perhaps you could listen to me sing, yes?"

We all look at our phones, worried about time.

But Jean-Pierre straightens himself and concentrates into the darkness, his eyes bulging. Then he opens his mouth and begins:

I shall sleep, I am lonely,
O Mama, O Papa, O loneliness!
When I was a boy, Mama called me from the door:
"Your father's home—please come inside,"
Although a year had passed since he had died.

"It's brutal," Corso says, glancing at me. "What a sad night. What the heck?"

"It is a song about loneliness and separation," Jean-Pierre croaks. "I wrote it as an opera about a boy who loses his father. True story. You kids with your hip-hop and rock-and-roll don't understand good music."

"You lost your dad?" I ask.

Jean-Pierre blinks his big frog eyes. "Yes, when I was ten. It was hard, monsieur, but soon I learned to let go. You have to learn, accept the past and move forward."

"You have a beautiful voice," Alice tells him.

Jean-Pierre proudly takes a bow and says, "If I could trouble you for one last favor. Would you kiss me and see if I turn back into a man?"

Moon and Alice both look at each other.

"Were you handsome?" Alice asks.

"I've been told I resemble Engelbert Humperdinck," he says.

Moon turns to me and shakes her head, then looks back at him. "Please," she says.

Jean-Pierre swallows hard, eyes bulging. "I mean Elvis."

"Huh?"

"*Baby*, you're wearin' that loved-on look, shoop shoop?"

"Whatever, let's get this over with," Alice says, and she and Moon both kiss him on the top of his head. Jean-Pierre's frog eyes fill with tears from happiness, or maybe gratitude. I wonder how long it's been since anyone has kissed him, or, for that matter, even talked to him. We stare at him, waiting for something to happen, for him to change into a man.

Jean-Pierre's bulging eyes look around, but nothing happens.

"Maybe it takes time," Alice says. "Maybe hours? Go to sleep and see if you wake up as a man."

"The spells are instant." He sighs. "I give up, mon amie. I must learn to live with the consequences. I cannot change things." Now he looks up at me with sadness. "But perhaps if you could—"

"Kiss you?" I say. "Fine, whatever."

I lean down and kiss the top of his head. Jean-Pierre's tongue slithers out of his mouth and then back inside. We wait for him to change, but again, nothing happens.

He looks up at Corso. "Mon ami?"

Corso sighs. "I knew it," he says. He leans down and kisses him also, but once again, nothing happens.

"Well, we've all kissed you," Corso says. "And nothing has happened, so this is all very awkward."

"See, there's no going back to the past," Jean-Pierre says. "There is no change back into a man, no return to my past life. I just have to accept that I'm a frog and move forward."

We all tell him goodbye, and then Jean-Pierre looks at me. "Just remember to keep moving forward," he croaks. "Accept the things you cannot change and work on the ones you can. I'm trying to do that, too. Sometimes it is all we can do, mon ami."

Then he hops across the road and disappears into the darkness, and we're all silent for a moment.

"We still need to figure out where we are," Alice says, but none of us can get a signal on our phones.

"Maybe we should get back on the horse and just ride?" I ask.

Moon points. "That way is west because you can see the lights of Poisonberry."

Just then we hear the crackling of tires from the gravel road and see headlights in the distance.

It's a car headed toward us.

(((16)))

Alice's Message

"Hey, I'm here!" a voice shouts from the car.

We see blinding headlights as the car approaches and comes to a stop. The engine is cut and the lights blink out. I'm terrified, wondering who found us out here, but then I see the door open and a man get out. As he comes forward, I hear Alice say, "Uncle Gaddith!"

It's Gaddith, thankfully. He hugs Alice and asks if we're all right.

"We're fine," she tells him. "What happened? How did you get away from the Raven Mockers? And whose car is that?"

"It's their car," Moon says. "It's the one Corso and I were in when they picked us up from the old gas station."

"You stole their car?" Alice shouts.

"I just borrowed it to escape," he says. "Also, it's a piece of junk."

"Also," Corso says, "they were going to cut out our

hearts and eat them. So I think taking their car was smart."

"Those old ravens chased me around the hill, but I could hear them wheezing. I saw their car parked with the keys in it, so I made a quick getaway."

"I'm glad you're safe," Alice says.

"It's been a weird night," I say.

Alice yawns, then the rest of us yawn after her. Yawning is contagious. This is proof.

"I think I want to go home," I say. "I can't take any more weirdness."

"We all need to go to bed," Moon says.

"I'll take you back to Poisonberry," Gaddith tells us. "Alice, can you ride Lampwick? I'll drive slowly so you can keep up. It's only a few miles."

"I will," she says, and he helps her mount the horse. The rest of us pile into the car, Corso in front, and me and Moon in the back.

Gaddith returns to the car and closes the door. "This thing is a real clunker," he says, turning the ignition. The car sputters as he revs the engine. We pull away slowly and head down the road. I turn around and see Alice and Lampwick following behind in the road dust.

"Are we safe?" Corso asks, yawning. "I'm ready to hit the sack."

A moment later he's snoring. Gaddith turns down a gravel road, and I hear sniffles. I look over to see that Moon is crying. It's weird to see her so upset by all this.

"What's wrong?" I say quietly. "What are you crying about?"

Moon wipes her eyes with her sleeve but doesn't look at me. "It's just that all along I knew this wouldn't work out."

"What do you mean?"

"There's no cave," she says. "No clues to help us find out what happened to Mom."

I feel my mouth go dry. Then I tell her that Alice already admitted to making up the story about a secret cave. "I know why she made it up," I tell her. "To feel special. And to try to help me. To help us."

Moon wipes her eyes again. "Aren't you disappointed?"

I look out the window into the darkness. I lean into the window and look up at the sky and see the moon's glow, forming a dark blue haze around it, and everything feels so quiet. I see the little stars swirling, and the crackle of gravel underneath the tires stops as we drive, as if the world falls silent for a moment to show me the moon's glow in the sky to cheer me up.

Yet I am afraid of something I cannot place. I'm worried I'll never find out anything about what happened to my mom, and that this whole night has been a series of disasters. A waste of time. What did we accomplish anyway? Moon and Corso almost got killed. I feel guilty about that, though I don't say anything to Moon.

We pass the desert gas station where we almost killed Andrew Jackson. I'm glad we didn't. Let the world take care of itself. Let the world heal and keep going forward. I would probably feel worse if we'd killed him, even if he deserved it.

Gaddith slows the car and stops at the edge of the road near Corso's neighborhood. He cuts the engine, and we all get out of the car. Alice isn't far behind us, on Lampwick, trotting until she reaches us and pulls the reins.

"Whooaaaa, Lampwick," she says.

Gaddith helps her down, and she tells us she had an interesting conversation with Lampwick during the ride home. "Poor Lampwick really is a sweet boy," Alice says.

We all stare at the horse. Then Lampwick turns his head and speaks to us.

"The fairy tale never ends," he says. "Look at me, once a fine young boy who just wanted to have fun. They worked me to death, to death I tell you. I suffered as jackass and now horse."

"You're no longer a jackass," Gaddith says. "You were disrespectful to your elders. You squandered your money by gambling and poisoned your lungs with smoke. What did you expect?"

Lampwick snorts, shakes his head. "To be honest, I prefer being a horse to a man. I'm me, that's who I am. I'm me and nobody else. I'm Lampwick, and I won't try to be something I'm not."

"That's the spirit."

Lampwick kicks his hoof against the dirt. "Be yourselves, kids," he snorts. "And do good things."

We all yawn out loud at the same time.

"Our cue to leave," Gaddith says. "Thanks for the adventure, everyone. I would've had a lonely night at home bingeing

Netflix. But instead I got to rekindle my love for Mina, and for that I thank you all."

"She's really pulchritudinous," I say.

Gaddith winks at me, then hugs Alice for a long time while the rest of us wait. "I love you, Uncle," she says. "I'll see you soon. Thank you for your help."

Gaddith mounts Lampwick and salutes us. "Lampwick's right," he says. "Do good things. I hope to see all of you again soon."

"Thank you, Gaddith," I say.

I know he probably feels sorry for me since we never found my mom, but I feel a strong sense of gratitude for all his help tonight. He kicks Lampwick into motion and they start back along the path, off into the dark desert.

"I always thought Pinocchio was a fairy tale," Corso says.

"Well, we didn't expect to see anything we saw tonight," Moon says.

I want to say something about not seeing Mom, but I hold back. And I feel like Moon does, too. We start walking toward Corso's house, none of us saying anything but all of us feeling, probably, that the night was a failure. Nobody wants to bring it up, so I just let it go.

Corso tells us bye when we reach his house. "The band is supposed to play the festival downtown this afternoon," he says. "It's almost sunrise—how will I stay awake when the time comes?"

"Go right to sleep," Alice tells him.

"But the band still needs a name. How will Bojack-Runt introduce us?"

"We'll figure something out," I tell him. "I'll meet you guys there before you play."

Corso takes a deep breath. "I'm worried it will be a disaster. See you there."

We watch him run to his bedroom window and ease it open. Then he hoists himself onto the ledge and crawls inside.

"It was a weird night," Alice says as we start down the street. "I'm not sure what to make of all of it. Maybe I'm just too tired."

"We're all tired," Moon says.

We walk in silence down the quiet and still street. When we reach the end of the block, Alice turns to us. "I have to tell you something before I leave," she says hesitantly. "It's something I've wanted to tell both of you all night."

"What is it?" Moon says.

Alice hesitates, then shakes her head. "It's nothing, never mind. I'll see you at the festival tomorrow."

"You mean today," I correct.

She hugs me, which feels good. I like that hugs feel good. Then she tells us goodbye before running down the street.

Moon and I keep walking toward our house. I think we're both unsure how we feel, whether it's disappointment or confusion or whatever. Maybe we're both too exhausted to feel anything this early in the morning. Moon asks me what I thought Alice was going to tell us.

"I don't know," I say. "Who knows?"

Moon suddenly stops walking.

"What's wrong?" I ask.

"Listen," she says. "Do you hear it?"

I don't hear anything at first, but then I hear a hoot.

"An owl?" I say. "Is that what you mean?"

We look around, but it's too dark to see anything, especially an owl. We start walking again, and Moon looks worried.

"It's just an owl," I tell her. "It's nothing to be scared of. Is that what you're worried about?"

"No," she says. "Don't you remember what Dad used to tell us? Those old stories about owls as messengers?"

"So what?"

"What do you think the owl is telling us?"

I think about this. "I don't know," I say.

When we finally reach our yard, Moon looks to the sky and says, "I think the sun's about to come up."

I look to the east, past the mountains on the horizon, where the sky is beginning to lighten. There's something about looking at the rising sun, peaceful on the horizon. The whole world is calm. I'm never up this early, but sometimes I like to sit outside while the sun sets in the distance. There's a calmness I like just before darkness falls. It feels like this right now.

I hear the birds, and I know the sun will rise soon. We stop at the porch and sit on the steps.

"Are you sad?" Moon asks.

"A little, I guess."

"Me too."

Then, suddenly, we hear a voice behind us: "Hello."

We both turn quickly around and can't believe what we see: Alice, sitting cross-legged on the porch under the front window.

"Alice!" we both say at the same time.

"Hello," she says again.

"Wow," I say. "How did you get here so fast? How did we not see you? And what are you doing?"

She laughs into her hands.

"I don't get it," Moon says. "We thought you went home?"

Alice stands and comes over in front of us on the steps. "I was going to, but I needed to tell you something first. I have a message for both of you."

Another secret, I think. What is it this time? What could possibly be worse than not finding out anything about our mom?

"More bad news," I say, looking at her. "Am I right? There's no cave and probably no clues to ever give us answers, I guess."

"That's probably true," Moon says.

In the moonlight, Alice's eyes look bright and fierce. A cool wind comes up momentarily, and beside us, some bush leaves rustle in the night breeze.

"The old traditional stories our grandparents tell," Alice says. "Do you believe them?"

Moon looks at me, but neither of us knows what to say or what she's getting at.

"Well," Alice continues, "I lost my sister many years ago,

remember? And when we never found out what happened to her, I decided I wanted to dedicate my life to helping others who feel like they have no story and are stuck. So that's what I've been doing tonight with you."

We both stare at her, speechless.

Finally, Moon says, "Huh?"

"I stopped looking for her when I realized I had stories to remember her by."

"Oh," Moon says, and we're all quiet for a moment.

"In the traditional stories, we are called Nunnehi," Alice says. "We live to protect each other from danger, and to help our own Cherokee people. And my job is that I want you to know that, even if you don't find any details about your mom, you have the stories your grandma has told you about her, which will keep you going. Your dad has stories, too. Many stories."

"Nunnehi," I say quietly. "Nunnehi?"

"Even spirits can't go back to the past and change it," Alice continues. "Nobody can. We can only go forward, just like Coyote and the frog said. And nobody will rob you of the memories of your mom—not even the Raven Mockers. I'll make sure of that."

"Nunnehi," Moon says. "Seriously?"

"Seriously. We must protect each other, and we must protect our stories. There are plenty of people who will tell lies about us. There are many who don't want our history to be a part of theirs. But we cannot give up. We take the truth of the past with us, and preserve it from being forgotten."

My heart is racing. "A Nunnehi," I say again. "Protector, shape-shifter."

"Close your eyes and count out loud to three," Alice tells us. "Go ahead, close them."

I look at Moon and we both close our eyes. Now my heart begins to beat even faster, and I can't contain myself, so I quickly open my eyes as soon as we count, "One . . ."

But Alice is already gone.

Moon and I don't say anything about what just happened. Alice disappeared right in front of us. Then I remember the story Grandma told me about the Nunnehi she knew when she was a little girl. I tell it to Moon now, and she lets out a long breath.

"Oh wow," Moon whispers, shaking her head. "I'm totally freaking out right now."

"Me too. I don't know what to even say," I tell her.

Moon stands and then quietly unlocks the front door and lets herself into the house, but I stay on the steps. I look out into the distance. I'm not sure what I feel. Everything that has happened tonight is beyond anything I imagined.

I can't sleep right now. I need to be alone because I haven't had hardly a minute to myself all night, which has felt overwhelming. I rub my hand over my eyes and yawn.

I hear an owl hoot in the elm tree in our yard. Is it the same owl we heard down the street? Did it fly over to our tree in the dark without us seeing it? Or is it a different owl?

I haven't thought about the owl stories Grandma used to tell us for a long time. In those stories, the owls brought important messages to the Cherokees. In one story, an owl witnesses a child's drowning in a river. The owl tries to swoop down and save the child but is unsuccessful. A dark spirit that watched the drowning tells the owl: "Go tell the boy's parents that their son has drowned," but the owl is too afraid.

"I don't want to be the one to deliver such sad news," the owl says.

The dark spirit laughs. "If you don't tell them, I will forever curse you and all owls from speech so that you will say only one pitiful sound. No one will know what you are saying and whether you are happy or sad."

So the owl flies to the boy's parents' house but is too afraid to tell them. When he returns, he admits to the dark spirit that he was too afraid.

Before he can try to plead, the spirit places the curse on him, and the owl can only hoot over and over.

I look up at the tree in our yard as the owl hoots.

What story is it trying to tell me?

(((17)))

Spiders from Mars

I wake to find Grandma staring at me, her face so close to mine I gasp.

"Do you always sleep this late on Saturdays?" she asks. "It's almost noon. Your dad got doughnuts this morning, but you and Moon wouldn't wake up to eat them."

I stretch, yawning. My eyes are heavy, and I feel groggy and lethargic. "Wait, it's noon? Seriously?"

"Hmm," she says. "You stayed up late playing video games, eh?"

I don't answer and instead get out of bed and hurry into my room, closing the door behind me. I look up at my poster of Michael Jordan. In the photo, he's flying over a player with his arm outstretched, about to dunk. His face is serious and intense yet inviting, and sometimes I talk to him.

"Life is weird," I whisper to him.

My phone beeps with a group text from Sheila: U guys ready for today?

Bojack-Runt: Meet by the stage at a quarter to two, guys.

Corso: Just woke up!

I text: Me too!

Vicious Sid:

Sheila: What is our band's name?

Bojack-Runt: We'll figure something out!

Corso: Something cool like Poison Viper.

Sheila: Lame.

Vicious Sid:

I get clean clothes out of my dresser and then go down the hall to the bathroom and take a shower. The warm water feels good on my body. While I shower, I think about everything that happened last night and all the people I met. I wonder whether Moon and I should mention it to our dad. Thinking about it still makes me a little sad, honestly, because I really thought I could find a way to see my mom again. I wonder why life is so unfair. Maybe I just have to accept that.

After my shower, I get dressed and hear the front door open. My dad comes in and sees me. His face looks worried, almost surprised.

"Are you feeling okay?" he asks.

"Yeah, why?"

"You slept late. I wondered if you were sick."

"No, I feel fine."

"Is Moon up yet?"

My grandma lights her pipe from the recliner. "She's still asleep. One of you should wake her."

"It's after noon," Dad says, walking past me to head to Moon's room.

I turn and watch him go down the hall. I can hear him talking to Moon, but I'm not sure what he's saying. A moment later he returns to the living room and sits on the couch.

"What's wrong?" Grandma asks him.

"Moon's supposed to cheer at the festival this afternoon," he says. "But now she's saying she doesn't want to. I don't know what's wrong with her."

"What did she say?" I ask.

"Just that she doesn't want to go."

It's not normal for Moon to say something like that, or not to go cheer. I wonder if she's just tired from the little bit of sleep we got. I head down the hall and knock lightly on her door, then open it. She's sitting up in bed with her back against the wall, doing something on her phone.

"Hey," she says, without looking at me. "What's up?"

"You're not going to the festival?" I ask her.

"No."

"Why not?"

She looks up at me. "Close the door," she says softly.

I step inside her room and pull the door behind me. I go over and sit down on the edge of her bed.

Moon sets her phone down. "Just as I was falling asleep this morning," she says, "I heard a tapping on my window. I sat up and saw a bird on the window ledge outside. It was a female cardinal."

I look at her window, then back at her. She looks tired, her eyes puffy and sleepy.

"She was such a pretty bird," Moon says, hooking a loose strand of hair behind her ear. "I opened the window and she flew inside."

"She flew into this room? How did you get it out?"

"She brought me a feather from Gus the buzzard. Can you believe it? Remember when Grandma used to tell us how much Mom loved the story about the Great Buzzard helping create the earth?"

"The buzzard story," I say. "Yeah, how the buzzard flew across the earth, using its wings to dig valleys and build mountains before flying back into the sky to join the other animals. What was the point of that story anyway?"

"To be nice to all creatures on the earth. And we were nice to Gus. If it was a test, we passed. This bird knew we met Gus. She flew in and wedged the feather into the molding above the door to keep the bad spirits away."

I look up and see a long brownish-white feather over the door.

"I don't know how to say this," she says, "so I'll just say it, Ziggy. The bird told me Mom is in a better place."

Moon is staring at me, and I can tell she's serious.

"It's somewhere better than here. Some other place where she can see us and watch us and make sure we're not feeling sad all the time. Mom doesn't want us to be sad all the time."

I don't understand.

"Do you remember when Grandma used to tell us stories about animals, and how when we treat them with kindness, they treat us kindly, too? Animals and people work together in harmony, which is the way it should be. And the cardinal helped me last night. What does it matter if I go to cheer? I always wanted to be the best cheerleader, but I never really liked cheering. So why do it, if it's only so I can try to win at it?"

I see what she's saying. But I still don't understand what she means by saying Mom's in a better place.

"I guess I don't know where Mom is," I say.

"Maybe it's a place where she watches us. Or maybe we can see her and don't realize we see her. Think about that."

I see the sunlight streaming in through her window, warming my legs. I have a sense of weariness and exhilaration, a trembling sensation of lightness. It's as if I don't even need to think about anything right now.

I go to my room and lie on my bed with my sketch pad. I draw shapes—circles, triangles, rectangles. I draw eyes and a mouth inside the shapes. I draw a pirate ship and an ocean with waves. I draw a giant eagle in the sky.

Soon Dad comes into my room and tells me it's time to go to the festival. He's wearing a ball cap and his sunglasses, ready to leave. "Do you want to go or stay here with Moon?"

"I want to go," I say. "Corso's band is playing, and I told them I would be there."

In the living room, Grandma lights her pipe from her recliner. She sits back and puffs in a cloud of smoke. "Enjoy the festival," she says, smoke drooling from her mouth.

"You're not coming?"

"I might show up later," she says. "Who knows? Gotta enjoy my midday smoke."

Dad opens the front door and I hurry after him to his truck. He starts the ignition and backs out of the driveway before I can even put my seat belt on.

"Dad, slow down," I say.

"What's the matter?" He doesn't seem to understand how bad his driving is, or how terrified I am by it.

"Dad," I say.

"What's wrong?"

Do you know that feeling of doing something scary for the first time? Like jumping off a diving board or getting into the car of a roller coaster? How your heart pounds and you feel hesitation near panic that's all fueled by fear? That's my ANXIETY. That's how I feel in the car with my dad, and now he can sense how much it's bothering me because he slows the car and pulls into a parking lot. He kills the engine.

I open my eyes and look at him. "I need to tell you something," I say. "But I don't want you to be mad. Okay?"

He reaches over and pats me on the shoulder. I hear him take a deep breath and exhale, then he runs a hand over his face. I'm worried I've irritated him, so I apologize.

"Don't apologize," he says. "What is it you want to tell me? You're not in trouble, are you?"

"No, it's about Mom."

We're on Mesquite Street, on the side of the road beside a small park. I see some kids climbing on playground equipment across the park.

"So," I continue, "last night Moon and I snuck out of the house to go to the desert to see if we could find a secret cave or a clue to help us locate Mom."

I close my eyes, worried my dad will start yelling, but he doesn't yell. I glance over at him and he doesn't even look mad. He takes a deep breath, and I can see the worry on his face.

"But nothing bad happened," I tell him. "I mean, we were safe."

"Well," he says, "your grandma and I were worried that would happen."

I turn and look at him. "You were? Why?"

"We just had a hunch," he says. "Did you find out anything?"

I look down at my hands and shake my head.

"It's fine," he says. "I still want to look for clues about what happened, too, but at some point we have to accept that there are some parts of the past we may never know."

"What do you mean?"

He runs a hand over his face again. "I mean we need to honor her by living our lives, not falling into the hole that appeared when she was taken from us. We can hold on to memories and use those to help us move forward. That's all we can do."

Up ahead, a woman walking a dog is crossing the street. She's talking on her phone and laughing. The sky is pale blue and cloudless.

"I'm sorry you get sad," he says. "I still get sad, too. And I miss Mom every day, but I think about the times we spent together before you were born and when you and Moon were babies, and that helps me."

"But I don't have memories of her. You have to give me some. I know you don't like to talk about it . . . but if you don't share what you have with me and Moon, Mom will disappear."

I can tell this hurts Dad a lot. But still, he nods.

"You're right. It's hard for me to do that . . . but I need to. You can have my stories and the ones Grandma tells you. There are other people who knew her, too. If we can't find your mother, we'll find more stories."

Through my window I can see the swing set in the park, and the merry-go-round, its metal glimmering from the sun. The silence between my dad and me fills the car with uncertainty until I feel him pat my shoulder, and I realize everything he has said makes sense.

"Let's grab a mocha inside," he says. "We can go into Beck's and get our drinks to go."

Beck's is a local coffee shop across the street from the park. We've been there many times because I like mochas. We get out and go inside, where the barista knows Dad by name. There's something I really love about getting coffee or doughnuts with my dad, especially when it's just the two of us. I feel closer to him, and I know it's his way of telling me he loves me. He's not great about expressing his emotions, but he shows me his love by taking me for a treat.

Back in the truck, I'm in a better mood, no longer feeling afraid or anxious. Dad's driving seems more careful, slower. As we turn down Main Street, a flock of birds scatters in front of us, and my dad says, "Your mom loved birds."

I don't say anything, but I watch the birds scatter into the sky.

I know my mom loved birds. She painted them, took photos of them. My dad always mentions it just about anytime we see a flock of birds.

This time, I ask him something I never asked him before. I wanted to leave him alone, but now I don't want to leave him alone.

"What was her favorite bird?" I ask.

And he says, "She really loved cardinals. She loved all birds, but she loved watching cardinals the most."

Dad drives downtown, where we park a few blocks away from the festival in the center square.

I look at the clock and see it's a quarter till two.

"We have to hurry!" I tell my dad. "The band plays at two on the stage."

I run ahead of him, knowing he'll understand and will get to the stage in time. I can already smell the meat cooking from the taco trucks, which I hurry past. I run past the booths selling homemade honey, fruit drinks, knickknacks, and jewelry, until I see Bojack-Runt and the others from the band standing by the main outdoor stage. By the time I reach them, I'm completely out of breath.

"Ed, where've you been?" Bojack-Runt asks. "We're up next and Corso isn't here. What'll we do?"

I see Sheila coming over. She hugs me and asks how I feel.

"I feel perfectly fine," I tell her. "Why do you ask?"

"This morning Corso texted me that you guys stayed out late," she says. "But I haven't heard from him since then."

"I'm worried he fell back asleep," Bojack-Runt says.

Sheila looks furious. "I knew I should've gone to his house and banged on his door," she says. "He's always late to everything. Did you guys know he has the school record for most tardies ever recorded in Poisonberry history? Like, ever?"

She immediately calls him, but it goes to voicemail.

"I'm introducing the band," Bojack-Runt says. "We've agreed on a name, just now."

"Just now?" I say. "What is it?"

"Ziggy and the Spiders from Mars," Sheila says.

Everyone looks at me.

"Seriously?" I say. "But I'm not in the band."

"That's what's so cool about it, right?" Sheila says. "And anyway, you might as well be a part of us."

"Be my co-manager," Bojack-Runt says. "I need help with this business. It'll be good to collaborate, Ed."

"Right on," I say, and we all hug. I've decided I like hugs and that I'll hug anyone who lets me from now on.

"They're waving us to the stage!" Sheila says. "What do we do?"

"We rock," Bojack-Runt says, and motions for them to follow him.

I stay to the side of the stage and look out at the people in the town square. Some are walking around, eating snow cones and hanging around the booths and taco trucks. My dad is talking to someone I can't see because the person's back is to me. It looks like an older man, maybe a friend.

Suddenly I hear screeching feedback from the microphone, which hurts my ears, and I see Mayor Simpleton tapping on the mic. He's wearing a polka-dot bow tie and sprightly red shirt. "Testing?" he says into the mic. "Can anyone hear me? Testing, one, two?"

Mayor Simpleton happens to look directly at me, and I give him a thumbs-up.

"Hello, everyone," he says. "Mayor Simpleton here, and I hope you're all enjoying the fall festival. We have a great lineup of activities today with lots of music, food, and fun. Sample the good food and support our local farmers and businesses here in Poisonberry. And now I'll turn it over so you can enjoy the music of some of our local students from Yona Middle School. And remember, folks—I know one thing, and that's I love you."

There are a few claps, but most people aren't paying attention. Bojack-Runt takes the stage, followed by Sheila, who sits at the drum kit, and Vicious Sid, who straps his guitar over his shoulder.

I'm terrified for all of them. I can feel my heart pounding. Bojack-Runt taps the mic and introduces himself. "I'm co-manager of the band, along with our newest co-manager slash member, Ziggy Echota. Ladies and gentlemen, please welcome Ziggy and the Spiders from Mars!"

He hurries off the stage and comes over to where I'm standing. I see the worried look on his face, and I know it's because Corso hasn't shown up. This could be a huge mess in front of all these people.

Sheila kicks the drum a few times to start a beat, then Vicious Sid starts thumping his bass guitar so that they have a rhythm going, but Sheila isn't singing. They just keep playing in rhythm. Bojack-Runt's eyes are closed and I think: *Oh no—it's a disaster!*

Then, out of nowhere, we hear the screech of Corso's guitar, and Bojack-Runt grabs my arm. "It's Corso—but where is he?" he asks.

We can't see him anywhere. I look out to the people and see them pointing to the sky, and Bojack-Runt says, "Look—it's him!"

I look up into the sky and see a giant hot-air balloon with Corso inside it, playing his guitar. There's someone next to him, but I can't see who it is. Everyone is looking up, even the band, as the hot-air balloon floats down and lands in the town square.

Corso is playing his guitar as he steps out of the door of the basket and makes his way to the stage. The entire downtown is now watching, even the people in office buildings who have opened their windows and are cheering. Construction workers in orange hard hats and vests are dancing.

Onstage, Corso and the band are playing their best song, "Jack White, Jack White!" Sheila sings. Corso and Vicious Sid are playing their guitars louder and better than I've ever seen them. They don't look anything like the band playing in Corso's garage.

When the song ends, the crowd erupts into applause. I've never seen so much excitement for my friends, which makes me laugh, and for an inimitable, buzzing moment, I am filled with an elusive feeling of happiness.

Then I see the person who was flying the hot-air balloon, and I can't believe who it is:

Grandma Moses!

My grandma was flying the hot-air balloon.

"Grandma?" I yell.

"What? Who's that?" Bojack-Runt says.

"My grandma!"

"What?"

"MY GRANDMA!" I yell.

Corso and Sheila and Vicious Sid all hurry over to us, breathing hard from adrenaline and post-performance excitement, and everyone is asking Corso how he managed to make such a remarkable entrance in the hot-air balloon.

Corso looks at me and says, "It's because of Grandma Moses."

I look over to see she's already back in the basket. The balloon is lifting from the ground.

"GRANDMA!" I yell again, hurrying across the square, but she doesn't hear me and is already floating away in the balloon. I watch her rise above the buildings and drift toward the clouds. I wave my arms and look around, but my dad isn't nearby either. Where did he go? Corso and the others rush over to me and start waving their arms, hoping my grandma will see us.

"She's too far away," I tell them. "Corso, tell me what happened."

(((18)))

A Visit

S o your grandma was on a motorcycle down the street from my house," Corso tells me as we walk toward the food trucks. "I saw her and waved her down. She told me she would give me a ride here since I was running late."

Bojack-Runt and Sheila and Vicious Sid have just left, and my dad's not answering the phone, so Corso and I are stuck with three dollars, enough to buy a taco and a drink to share.

"But my grandma doesn't ride a motorcycle," I say.

"Are you kidding? She has the coolest bike I've ever seen. Saddlebags, stereo, a skull and crossbones painted on it, and her name: GRANDMA MOSES."

I can't believe it. I call my dad again and still get his voice-mail, so I leave him another message: "Dad, I'm by the food trucks. Where did you go?"

"Anyway, she gave me a ride to the airport and told me she was taking the hot-air balloon for a quick spin."

"How does she even know how to fly one?"

We both look into the sky. The sun warms our cheeks, tight with dry air. A moment later my dad calls.

"I'm inside the coffee shop, talking to Bud Ridley," he says. "I'll be out in a few minutes."

"Did you see Grandma?" I ask, but he's already hung up.

"It was so amazing," Corso says. "That was the most incredible feeling ever." He laughs at himself. "Did you guys totally freak out?"

I laugh, too, awkwardly. I can't believe it, and there are too many questions. Why did Grandma fly a hot-air balloon? Why didn't I know she could ride a motorcycle? And where did she even *get* a motorcycle?

"Bojack-Runt and me, we couldn't believe it," I say.

Corso laughs again.

"I have to go home and talk to her," I say.

I hear a whistle and my dad calling my name. He's across the street, walking out of the coffee shop. I turn to Corso. "Hey, you need a ride home?"

"Nah, but let me know what your grandma says. If it really was her, I want her to take us up in that balloon again."

My dad crosses the street, and I run to meet him as we head for the truck. "I was talking to my old pal Bud Ridley," he says, "so I missed your friends' band."

"You didn't see Grandma?" I say. "Grandma was flying a hot-air balloon!"

"Well, I'm not surprised," my dad says. "It's a hobby of hers.

She rides motorcycles as well. She's even in some biker gang of retired women. It's pretty cool. They ride all over the country when she's feeling well enough."

My dad is walking at a quick pace and I try to keep up with him. He shakes his head, laughing, saying he can't believe he never told me this.

"That's one of the coolest stories I've ever heard," I tell him. "And I've heard lots of stories over the past couple of days."

Back home, Grandma is smoking her pipe and sitting in her chair. "Yep, bikes and hot-air balloons," she says. She crosses her legs, and I see her black motorcycle boots.

"I can't believe it," I tell her. "Why didn't you ever tell me?"

"I prefer to tell you stories about your mom," she says. "But I can tell you hot-air balloon and motorcycle stories if you want. I once rode from Oklahoma to California and back with my group of friends. We were wild hippies."

"A long time ago, huh?"

"Last year," she says. "I felt well enough for an adventure, and what a fun trip it was. We're planning another next summer."

I look at my dad and see the lines etched around his eyes, furrows marked on him from all his worries, but right now he looks happy.

"You have stories, too," he says. "Think of all the memories you have and tell them the best way you can." I think about this. I see myself as a little boy, age five, standing in front of him and holding a toy snake I told him was a real one I saved from dying underneath a rock. At age six, showing him an invisible raccoon named Theodore, who could whistle in perfect timing the tune to "You Are My Sunshine." At age eight, tossing magical dust into the air that rains down, healing us so that we don't have to feel sad anymore.

"I'm going to work in the backyard," he says, and heads out the back door, leaving me alone with Grandma.

I see the smoke clear from around her, revealing her face, her blue hair hanging down past her shoulders. I feel a new closeness to her like never before, even more drawn to her soul and pierced by her longing to tell stories.

So I tell her the story of everything that happened last night. It all comes pouring out of me like a confession, from wanting to find a secret cave to meeting Rango, from Gus to Gaddith, from Andrew Jackson to the Raven Mockers, to all the other characters we met, and finally, walking back home to discover Nunnehi are real.

When I finally finish talking, my grandma lights her pipe. "You're a storyteller, too," she says. "And I think you learned a great deal you haven't realized yet. Can you write down what you learned?"

"I'll do it right now," I tell her. I go to my room and close the door. I look at the poster on my wall of Michael Jordan flying toward the rim. He turns his head and says, "Dude, you learned a lot."

"Like what, Michael?" I ask.

"Think about it. Think about everyone you met and what they told you."

I lie back on my bed and stare at the ceiling. My eyes are still heavy from staying out so late, but it's too late in the day for me to fall asleep, and I think about everyone I met and what they told me. I go over to my desk and open my notebook and write:

THINGS I LEARNED LAST NIGHT:

FROM GUS, THE BUZZARD:
It's good to be different.

FROM ANDREW JACKSON, THE ARMADILLO:
Violence is rarely justified, and violence by those who have power is almost always wrong.

FROM PETER O'DOUL:
Forgiveness must be genuine, not just a way of freeing yourself from guilt.

FROM MINA MINOMA AND GADDITH:
Falling in love is a type of magic we have to experience for ourselves.

FROM BELA LUGOSI:
Not all snakes are dangerous. Some can be generous.

FROM THE RAVEN MOCKERS:
Be careful whom you trust.

FROM JEAN-PIERRE LE PEU (FROG) AND
LAMPWICK (HORSE):
We must accept there is no turning back time.

Grandma was right—it's so obvious. I take my notebook back into the living room and read her everything I wrote.

"Very good," she says. "See what you learned? You have to learn to like yourself, Ziggy. And accept that you can't go back to the past and change things. Storytellers have power, Ziggy. We find the meaning in what's happened, and then we convey that meaning to others."

My phone buzzes, and I see that it's Alice. I've been waiting to talk to her all day. Is she really a Nunnehi? Everything feels like such a blur. I step onto the front porch and answer it.

"Sorry I didn't make it to the festival today," she says. "I fell back asleep."

"I can't wait to tell you about it."

"Why don't you come over? My mom and dad say they want to meet you."

I decide to ride my bike to Alice's rather than walk. I haven't ridden in a long time, and I'm still exhausted from little sleep, so my legs are feeling weak. I pass La Nueva Casita restaurant and the bushes of poisonberries beside it. I ride past the park and Real Inx tattoo, where Moon says she will someday get a tattoo of a phoenix on her shoulder. Then I go past the old abandoned Sol Grocery and Grill building with its mural of a handshake and an Octavio Paz quote above it that my dad has memorized: *Deserve your dream.* I go past the old adobe structures and houses, and finally I make it to Alice's street, where I have to swerve to miss the poisonberries until I reach her driveway.

I see Alice at the door, and I think about all her glittering acts of kindness, what makes the Nunnehi swell with power. Is it possible she really is a Nunnehi? Or am I searching for a friend or a protector, someone whom I've longed to be a best friend my whole life? Is it possible we're both such outcasts that neither of us can truly understand what it means simply to understand our own individual stories? Our own culture and history?

She comes outside as I park my bike. "Hey, are you freaked out by what I told you?"

"About being a Nunnehi?" I say. "A little, I guess. But don't worry, it's all good."

"I feel like I need to tell you more so you'll understand. Are you okay?"

I'm yawning, really tired, but I explain everything that's happened all day, and she looks bewildered. "Your grandma can ride a motorcycle *and* fly a hot-air balloon?"

"Is that cool or what? I had no idea."

"Amazing," she says.

I follow her into the house, where her parents are sitting in the living room. Alice's mom introduces herself. Their home smells of fresh pine and is elaborately decorated with antiques and lots of art on the wall. If they really are Nunnehi, they have expensive tastes. There's a cabinet full of antique china and intricately designed glassware. Alice's dad is reading a newspaper. As he stands to greet me, his overall stature is tall and intimidating, but he has a look of sincerity.

"This is Ziggy," Alice tells her dad. "Ziggy, this is my dad."

He shakes my hand. "Siyo, Ziggy," he says in a quiet voice.

"Come sit here on the couch," Alice's mom says, and picks up a photo album. "I want to show you some pictures of Andrea and the family."

"You remember I told you about my sister, Andrea?" Alice says.

"Yeah."

I'm sitting on the couch with Alice's mom between Alice and me. I lean forward with my hands in my lap while she flips through the photo album. Their living room is cozy and warm with a large window that overlooks their yard.

"What do you think of my birdbath?" Alice's mom asks, pointing outside. I look out the window, where some birds are preening themselves on her birdbath. "It's my favorite thing about the yard. We like to sit out there a lot. See the birds out there? Aren't they nice?"

"Yeah," I say, "I like it."

"Just *look* at them, Ziggy. Alice, remember when Andrea used to love to watch them?"

Alice nods.

"Do you like birds, Ziggy? I love sitting here and watching them. I saw a really pretty blue jay this morning."

"I prefer to watch vintage MTV," Alice's dad says. "Vintage videos. Either that or we play music and dance."

I think about how the Nunnehi love to play music, which is what Grandma always said in her stories.

"Alice can dance," her mom says.

I find Alice's parents funny. They offer me a lemonade and chocolate bunny cookies that Alice's mom said she made, so I immediately feel at home. Alice's mom takes my hand and pats it while I eat a chocolate bunny.

"There's another girl who disappeared recently," she says. "Her name's Gena, from Bernalillo. And another named Paula, from Las Cruces."

Alice's dad brings his hands together as if clasped in prayer and leans forward. "We read about that in the paper," he says. "It's really sad. It's terrible. Maybe we can help. We're trying to."

"I told them about your mom," Alice says to me. "We all have missing loved ones."

"I'm so sorry to hear it," Alice's mom says. "You have to pray and keep faith that everything will get easier for you. It's what we still do. We just have to learn to accept it."

She opens the family album in her lap. "I still keep Andrea's bedroom exactly the way it was when she was here with us. We've kept all her things, her stuffed animals and toys and clothes the way they were." She looks up from the album. "Sometimes I hear things in the middle of the night. Knocks, noises, things being hammered. I don't know how many times Frank has gotten out of bed to check on things."

I'm not sure what she's getting at, but the way Alice's dad is shaking his head seems like he knows Alice's mom is having a hard time. "I noticed chipped areas on the wood of the coffee table that only just appeared," she says. "We hear knocking late at night."

"We've had this coffee table for fifteen years," Alice's dad adds. "It's never once been moved from this spot. It was never bumped or hit or banged around. What are we supposed to think?"

"It's Andrea's spirit," Alice says.

"I want to believe it's Andrea's spirit," her mom says. "Maybe it's weird to say that, but I know somewhere in the back of my mind that she's here."

"She was always so active, is the thing," Alice's dad says. "That coffee table is old and needs to be replaced." He looks at his wife. "I can't explain the chipped wood."

There's a scratching at the back screen door, and Alice gets up and lets a cat inside. She picks it up and strokes under its chin. "This is Liza," she says, manipulating its paw to wave at us. "For a long time, Mom thought Liza was Andrea."

"Andrea named her," her mom says. "She always walked around carrying Liza and talking to her. We talk to Liza here, too."

"Sometimes we hear music," Alice's mom says. "But it stops the moment I get up to put on my robe. Alice never hears a thing, being such a heavy sleeper. But Andrea had a silly side to her, which is why I believe it's her. She used to take piano lessons, and sometimes at the piano, right in the middle of a song, she'd just all of a sudden start banging on the keys with her elbows."

"She was only eleven," Alice's dad says.

Suddenly, everyone falls quiet. I find myself looking around the room, unsure what to say. "I guess I should probably head back home," I say, and Alice's mom puts her hand on mine.

"Please stay," she says. "We haven't had much company lately. We would like it if you would stay for dinner."

Alice's dad lights a cigarette. He blows a long stream of blue smoke, which lingers in front of him. "Sure, stay for dinner," he says.

Their grief appears in the dark puffiness under their eyes and in the way they speak of Andrea with such a delicateness, as if they are struggling to put the past behind them. I feel like I can totally understand that.

Then Alice's mom says, "You have such pretty hair. May I brush it?"

I glance at Alice, who is looking down at the floor. I can't tell what she's thinking, so I nod.

"Sure," I say, and she reaches for the brush from the coffee table and begins brushing my hair. It feels good to let her do this for some reason. It doesn't make sense and seems sort of crazy. I mean, how many of my friends' parents pay attention to me, much less have a long conversation and want to brush my hair? But it's good for us because maybe we all need a little help understanding things.

So I close my eyes and let Alice's mom brush my hair. She begins humming a tune that sounds familiar, and for a moment I think I hear music playing in another room.

(((19)))

Yellow Butterflies

Outside, Alice thanks me for coming over. "Sorry if my parents seem weird," she says.

We both think that's funny. "Yeah, it's fine. I promise, next time I'll stay for dinner. Remember what Gus said last night? Weird is good."

"Right," she says, "but I'm worried you're mad at me. I hope you don't think it was a waste of a night."

"Why?"

"Because I lied to you, Ziggy. I lied to you and said I knew for sure there was a secret cave. I wanted you to trust me. I don't have any friends really except you. Everyone calls me Weird Alice, remember?"

"So what?"

"Well," she says, "I had fun with you last night."

"Yeah, I'm glad we're friends," I tell her.

On the bike ride home, I see some kids by the park jumping

over the poisonberries. I feel exhilarated. I see a line of blackbirds swoop over the high steeple of a church, then over telephone wires and the tops of houses, flying east toward the mountains in the distance. I pedal hard, gliding on my bike down the street, past a broken soda bottle gleaming in the sun, breathing damply with anticipation like I'm about to plunge into a lake.

Up above, the sky is vast blue, and I see a small white cloud with its edge trailing off into all that empty blueness, a single cloud hanging motionless and alone. There is so much to that cloud, I feel, so much to the blueness, as if nothing is everywhere and everything is nothing, vanished in all that vastness of blue above me.

I keep riding down the street, pedaling hard, exhilarated with an energy I didn't think I could have after so little sleep. The way everything looks when I'm this tired is strange, as if the sunlight slants in a blur of yellow shards like glass. I hear birds chirping and screeching in the trees as I ride past them. Yellow and white butterflies, dozens of them, are beating their wings along the side of the road.

By the time I make it back home, I can smell the chicken my dad is grilling in the backyard. I see the white smoke from the cooker drifting over the house and into the wind. I go inside and wash my hands and face in the bathroom.

In the mirror's reflection, very suddenly, I see Moon standing behind me. She is standing in a long T-shirt with a cartoon bear on it and yawning as if she just woke up. I turn around and look at her.

"Did you just wake up?" I ask her.

"Sort of. How was the festival?"

"It was fun. Corso showed up in a hot-air balloon."

"Did Grandma fly it?"

"Wait, you knew?" I say. "You knew Grandma can fly a hot-air balloon?"

"Of course."

"Did you also know she rides a motorcycle?"

"Yeah, of course," she says, stepping back so that she can see herself better in the mirror. "Are you feeling better today?"

I turn on the cold water and splash it on my face, then dry off with a hand towel beside the sink. "What a day. What a night. Think of all the stories we've collected."

"Grandma always says that stories heal us, remember? We should all be storytellers."

"Do you think Alice is really a Nunnehi?" I ask.

Moon looks at me in surprise. "Don't you believe it? After everything else?"

"I thought Mom was immortal."

"Grandma says only the Nunnehi are immortals," she says. "But the rest of us have to learn and struggle, even with their help."

She stretches, smiles at me in the mirror, then heads back down the hallway to her bedroom.

I turn off the light in the bathroom and then step outside to the backyard, where my dad is finishing up grilling chicken. He looks up and asks if I'm hungry.

"A little," I say. "But can I ask you something?"

"Sure."

I sit down on the steps. "I know we talked earlier about this, but you think she's dead, don't you? I mean, I'm pretty sure she's not coming back."

My dad uses a spatula to set the chicken breasts on a plate. For a moment I think he's ignoring me, but then he puts the spatula down and turns to me.

"Ziggy," he says, and though he can't seem to finish his thought, I know exactly what he wants to say, that it's very likely my mom has passed away and is never coming back. That after so many years our hope learns to accept what is most difficult for us and what makes us stronger people. We have to believe that justice will be served in the end, and that we will one day see her again, in this world or the next.

My dad takes a deep breath, muttering something else, and I stop him so that it's no longer so painful for him to talk about. It's painful for everyone, and maybe that pain never goes away. Maybe it never gets easy.

"Ziggy," he says again. "You know your mom loved birds. She also liked to go for long walks with her camera and take photos of butterflies. I remember once we drove up in the mountains and went for a hike, and she took photos of a stream, the mountains, cacti, clouds. She would take photos and then immediately show them to me on her camera and ask, 'What do you think? Do you love it?' She always wanted my opinion, but I thought all her photos were beautiful. She took a photo of a string of butterflies batting their wings like crazy. It was one of my favorite photos she took, with the mountains and blue sky in the background. We took lots of walks along trails back then. It was always just the two of us, so peaceful and quiet. She really loved doing that."

"I remember you told us she liked butterflies. But now I know much more than that. Thank you."

He falls quiet, like he's deep in thought. Or maybe I've made him sad. "Can you go inside and set the table for dinner?" he asks. "And wake up Grandma."

I go inside, but Grandma is already setting the table, a cigarette drooping from her mouth. Her hair is up in a bun, and she's wearing a flowery type of dress with motorcycle boots.

"I'm going for a bike ride tomorrow afternoon," she tells me. "I'm thinking about riding down to El Paso and back. You wanna go with me?"

She takes a drag on her cigarette and blows a thin stream of blue smoke.

"Maybe," I say. "Yeah, that would be fun."

"Groovy," she says. "We'll get you a biker jacket to wear like mine."

I hear her hoarse laughter turn into coughing as she disappears into the kitchen.

That night after everyone is in bed, I realize sometimes you just have to accept that things aren't the way they seem, like me finding out Grandma rides a motorcycle and flies a hot-air balloon, or that so many animals out there tell stories we need to hear, or that you can't understand the past. Nobody can ever change things that happened in the past. I'll just keep going to school like everyone else and hope for the best.

In the silence, I hear a sudden, light knock at the window. I sit up from the couch and peek from behind the curtain to see Alice standing on the porch. She waves me outside, so I put on my hoodie and step outside onto the front porch.

She's standing there, twirling her hair and looking up into the sky.

"It's so dark tonight," she says. "Wanna see the stars?"

"What are you doing here?" I say. "It's late. Don't your mom and dad know you sneak out?"

She looks at me and laughs.

I sit down on the porch steps, and she sits beside me. "You're funny," she says.

"Well, I can't go on another adventure tonight," I tell her. "I'm exhausted from so little sleep. I'm going straight to bed."

"We don't need to go on any more adventures," she says. "You have a good home with your dad and Moon and your grandma. There's no need to really look for clues to find your mom."

"You don't think there are any clues out there?"

I think about this. I look down at my feet, then at Alice's. She's wearing thick socks with tiny puppies on them, and I wonder why she didn't wear shoes to walk all the way over here. Surely that would tear her socks, but they look perfect.

"You've been too worried, too stuck on the past," she says.

"Moon and I both wanted to find her."

"I know," Alice says. "Everyone who loses someone wants to move time backward, but obviously we can't do that. We can only keep hope. But she is here with you. She will always be with you, Ziggy."

She stands and starts to walk away.

"Wait," I say. "Where are you going?"

She turns, twisting her hair. "Home," she says. "I'm going home, Ziggy."

I watch her walk, almost glide, into the darkness.

For a moment I sit out there, thinking she'll come back, but she doesn't. I'm so tired I can barely keep my eyes open, so I step back inside and lie down on the couch and fall fast asleep.

When I wake in the morning, it's sunrise and I can't fall back asleep. I sit up. The house is silent, everyone else still sleeping.

I stretch and yawn, then go over to the front window. I can hear the birds chirping outside, where yellow butterflies are beating their wings furiously. This is how the rest of my life can be, I think: standing by a window and looking outside, missing my mom. Maybe I will sleepwalk into the kitchen, expecting to find her sitting there eating honey on toast, like she used to do on nights she couldn't sleep. My dad once said he liked to watch her wash the vegetables and potatoes in the sink. She shaved carrots, chopped onions, used a boning knife on the catfish he'd caught from the lake.

I think: Maybe I could call out for my mom.

Don't be afraid, she would tell me. *Live your life.*

Author's Note

When I began writing this book, I knew I wanted to write something for my kids about anxiety. Several years ago, I taught seventh-grade English for a short time, and one thing I noticed about those middle school years is how difficult, scary, and strange they are for so many kids. I remember those years as especially difficult when I was twelve or thirteen.

Once I started drafting the book, as I thought more about anxiety, I also thought about what it means to lose someone. In the US, we're currently living in dangerous times, with repeated school shootings and a deadly pandemic. How do kids deal with loss? I've always thought about how hard it must be for Native kids whose mothers, sisters, aunts, and grandmothers go missing. Because of this ongoing crisis, kids are left without many answers. So I began thinking about how they're able to handle their anxiety, and how they manage hope, forgiveness, and acceptance.

While these are all serious issues, I also wanted the book to be fun and, hopefully, engaging these issues with fun references to music, Shakespeare, and wild imagination. Wilma Mankiller, the first woman Chief of the Cherokee Nation, once said, "The most fulfilled people are those who get up every morning and stand for something larger than themselves." My hope is that *The Storyteller* inspires readers to think about and stand for something larger than themselves.

—Brandon Hobson

Sources

Some words are taken from the *Cherokee-English Dictionary* by Durbin Feeling, published in 1975 by the Cherokee Nation of Oklahoma, edited by William Pulte.

Part of the armadillo's speech is taken from Andrew Jackson's second annual address to Congress in 1830.

Acknowledgments

My thanks go to Bill Clegg and everyone at the Clegg Agency. Thank you, David Levithan, for helping me shape this book, and thanks to everyone at Scholastic. Thank you, Sharon Steinborn. Thanks to the UCROSS Foundation. For the cover, thanks to Natasha Donovan, Elizabeth B. Parisi, and Nicole Medina. Finally, thanks to my family, as always. Wa'do.

About the Author

Dr. Brandon Hobson is a 2022 Guggenheim fellow. He received his PhD from Oklahoma State University and is the author of four books for adults, including the recent novel *The Removed*. His novel *Where the Dead Sit Talking* was a finalist for the National Book Award, among other distinctions. His short stories have won a Pushcart Prize and have appeared in *The Best American Short Stories*, *McSweeney's*, *Conjunctions*, *NOON*, and elsewhere. He teaches creative writing at New Mexico State University and at the Institute of American Indian Arts and is an enrolled citizen of the Cherokee Nation Tribe of Oklahoma. Dr. Hobson lives in New Mexico with his wife and two kids.